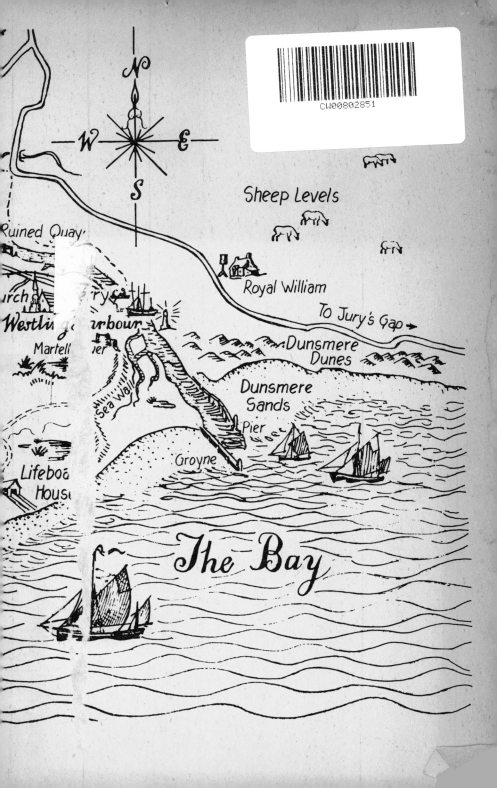

STRANGERS
TO THE MARSH

"He couldn't help it!" Tamzin was saying earnestly. "Oh, do be careful Jim, you shoved your elbow right in the middle of that walnut cake. Come out slowly!"

"But what about my cakes?" cried the baker wringing his hands, "a small fortune's worth – all spoilt, all smashed – and what about the mess in my van?"

And that's how the adventure started. How to pay the baker for the gorgeous cream cakes and jam puffs Old Jim the Ferryman squashed when the *Emma,* his ancient bicycle – suitably adorned with anchors and fenders – ran away down the steep hill and crashed into the baker's van? Tamzin and her friends Rissa, Meryon and Roger decide to compile and sell a newsheet of local news to help Jim raise the cash – and it does well. But its success turns to near-tragedy when they print the story of the arrival of a family of rare birds – hoopoes at Cloudesley Castle. Much to the amateur reporters' distress, crowds of well-meaning but ignorant sightseers turn up, bussed in by the obnoxious Hookey Galley – and the disturbance nearly causes the hoopoes to desert the nest. Then, to crown it all, the solitary young hoopoe chick mysteriously disappears.

*To Stephen B. Fry, enterprising editor
of The Buckler's Hard News since his
tenth year; and to Elizabeth Macfie,
who knew the hoopoes*

AUTHOR'S NOTE

Although written some time afterwards
this book is meant to come, in sequence
of time, just before *Hidden in a Dream*.

STRANGERS
TO THE MARSH

A *Romney Marsh* Story

MONICA EDWARDS

JOHN GOODCHILD PUBLISHERS
AYLESBURY

John Goodchild Publishers,
10 Mandeville Road,
Aylesbury,
Buckinghamshire,
HP21 8AA

John Goodchild Publishers is an imprint of
BOOKWARD LTD.

First published in this revised edition 1986
© Copyright Monica Edwards 1957, 1986

Revised by the author.
Cover illustration by Gordon King.
Cover design by Sue Harris.

British Library Cataloguing in Publication Data
Edwards Monica
    Strangers to the Marsh.——New, rev. ed.——
    (Romney Marsh adventures)
  I. Title   II. Ratcliffe, Sheila   III. Series
  823'.914[J]   PZ7
  0 86391 074 2

Set in 11 on 14pt Times by Trintype
Printed by Nene Litho
Bound by Woolnough Bookbinding
All of Irthlingborough, Northants

CONTENTS

CHAPTER 1

The Scuppering of the *Emma*

No other houses could look as unreal as Dunsford houses did late on a still June afternoon, Tamzin thought. She and Rissa, going home from school, stood talking at the top of the hill where presently Rissa would turn off down West Street to her home in Dunsford town, and Tamzin would cautiously push her old bicycle down the cobbles of Mermaid Street's sharp gradient before mounting at the Strand and setting off on her two-mile journey over the Marsh to Westling Vicarage.

"I suppose it's looked just like this for hundreds of years," Tamzin was saying, staring at the familiar loved houses crowding down the hill in a jumble of sun-warmed tiles and bricks and timber, "except that the sea was at the Strand."

"What I was saying *was*," said Rissa, "that as today's Friday there isn't any rush about homework——"

"I know," said Tamzin apologetically. "I did hear, really. Yes, do come down after tea – or now, if you like: Mother never minds. But you'd better dash in and tell yours as she'll be expecting you."

"Are you going to wait here?" Rissa asked, swivelling on the ball of one foot.

"Yes, I've got to tighten up the string that holds my mudguard on, and my saddle's slipped again.'

Rissa laughed with a sudden snort. "If I had such a medieval machine as yours, I'd rather borrow old Jim's *Emma*. He hardly ever uses her."

"He does; he's dug her out again, and what's more he's in Dunsford with her now. I saw him pedalling along Cinque Ports Street when we were coming up through the Land Gate and I said so, but you were looking at the horse in the forge. I do wish he wouldn't."

"Wouldn't what?"

"Go wobbling about on that awful old bike. It's just ridiculous trying to learn a thing like that at his age, and you know what happened last time."

"To begin with," said Risa reasonably, "nobody really knows his age; and to middle with, we gave him the *Emma* ourselves; and to end with, I dare say he needs a change from rowing the ferryboat as much as we need one from school. I won't be five minutes – would you like me to bring you another piece of string? But honestly, what youɪ bicycle really needs is a hole in the ground."

"It isn't a case of new string; it's a case of getting this string tight. I'll get Dad to put a piece of wire round it. . . ." But Rissa had gone. Tamzin looked at her mudguard with a kind of baffled distaste, and then back at the golden quietness of the afternoon where it was held between the houses, almost as if it were a pale yellow river running slowly down the cobbles to the Strand. The heat dithered in the middle of the air above it, like mayflies over the water. A baker's van which had stopped at the bottom of the street looked like a boat under water, its sides distorting slightly under the sun. But the van had broken the enchantment of the deserted street and Tamzin leaned once more over her mudguard. She actually had her fingers on the mud-sealed knot when a strange approaching rattle made her look up again. It was coming from the direction of Church Square, and though nearly everything rattled on Dunsford's cobbles it sounded remarkably like the old ferryman's bicycle, on which he had hung various seaman-like things such as an anchor and fenders and a lantern. Tamzin leaned on her handlebars until a sudden outbreak of white hair and beard round the corner confirmed her expectations.

"Hey, Jim! It's me, Tamzin!"

The old man would never have seen her. He was far too preoccupied with piloting his vehicle round the worst eruptions of cobbles. But the unexpected sound of her voice made him suddenly glance up.

"Gor, bless us, sink me if it ent young Tamzin!"

"Oh, do be careful, Jim!" Tamzin shouted anxiously. "You ought really to *walk* down here."

"Dah, bollar it, I reckon I ent that soft yet," the ferryman bawled back, his voice jumping out of him with the jumpiness of the cobbles. "I reckon 'er be all right if so I can git her up on the pavement, gal." Recklessly, he took a hand off the upright handlebar to wave to Tamzin as he clattered past and in so doing swerved his front wheel against the kerb. For the next two minutes Tamzin hardly knew what she or Jim were doing at all. Looking back afterwards there was a hazy impression of a furiously leaping, bucking, rocketing bicycle, all mixed up with strong seafaring oaths and shining, blowing hair and beard. Tamzin herself was running urgently down the steep curving hill, having presumably done something with her own bicycle first – and the quiet dreaming windows were sprouting wide-eyed faces.

9

Down at the bottom of the street the baker had just left his van. He was only going round to the back door of one house and Dunsford is an honest, clean town, so he had seen no reason to shut his double doors. Inside the van the floor was piled with a foam of Dunsford's finest, creamiest cakes and pastries, like a fat child's dream of heaven. Tamzin saw the fluff and crunchiness and jamminess of them in the same glance as she saw where Jim's bicycle was heading.

"Scuttle 'er for a coghead!" the old man was roaring as he hurtled down past the leaning old houses, "'er wunt answer to the helum, nor yet to the anchor, neether."

And then suddenly, like a small bomb in a cloister, the inevitable crash came, and old Jim was somehow diving into the middle of the foaming pastries, and Tamzin was pulling away the wilting bicycle to get at Jim, and the baker was pulling at her to get at both of them, and the noise of eager spectators approaching made the perfect peace of Mermaid Street sound like a stamping ground of buffaloes.

This was what Rissa saw when she turned the corner from West Street, pushing her bicycle. Not that she could really recognise whose sea-booted legs they were, waving in the doorway of the baker's van; but since the person with the long fair hair was obviously Tamzin, and the wreckage at the roadside was almost as obviously a rather nautical bike, it seemed reasonable to suppose that it was Jim inside the van; though why he should be, Rissa's logical mind simply boggled to imagine. Pushing her bicycle on to the smooth runway of the pavement, she jumped on and swooped anxiously down the hill.

From his bed of rich cakes the ferryman's voice came out in a thickly muffled volley of strong language such as Tamzin and Rissa had hardly heard before in all their years at Westling Harbour. The baker was nearly crying, hardly knowing whether to salvage the few of his cakes that had escaped the disaster, or to help extract this large and floundering sailor who was grovelling in the midst of them, or whether even to slam the double doors on the lot and rush home screaming.

"He couldn't help it!" Tamzin was saying earnestly, "I'm sure he couldn't help it. Oh, do be careful, Jim, you shoved your elbow right in the middle of that walnut cake, then. Come out *slowly*!"

"An' how in tarnation d'ye think I know if I'm coming or going?" roared Jim. "When me eyes is larded up wid cream? Gor, darn take it, I never saw the like, scupper me if I did."

"Oh! My beautiful cream puffs! Take his hulking great boot out of them, someone, for pity's sake!" cried the baker, who always personally delivered his own creations rather than entrust them to anybody else.

"Crumbs! What a mess," said Rissa, thrusting her bicycle up against a medieval wall.

"Crumbs is the right word, lass," said a spectator appreciatively.

"Now listen, Jim, stop flailing about and put your left foot *here*," said Rissa firmly, "and then your right one here."

There was a loud spluttering noise as the ferryman suddenly blew, and fresh cries broke out from the baker as a blizzard of jammy cream came to land in scattered places. "All over my little Tea Loaves!" he mourned, "that were ordered for Lady Siskin's party."

"He's nearly out now," Tamzin said soothingly. "Careful, Jim – now you can put your feet down on the road. Phew!" she added, as at last the old man stood up squarely in front of her, but just as suddenly he sat down again on the van.

The baker shrieked and Tamzin cried out, "Not on all those cakes again, Jim!"

"If you must sit down," said Rissa, "sit in the road."

"Once squashed is squashed for good," said Jim. "I bin and hurt me ankle, that's what I done. And it takes more time to make an ankle nor what it does a batch of fancy cakes. Crippled meself for life, I shouldn't wonder, at my age, and what sympathy do I git?"

"D'you think we ought to send for an ambulance?" Tamzin said to Rissa doubtfully.

"I ent gooing to ambulate for no-one," Jim said, sticking out his white beard doggedly. "Nor I wunt go into hospital, neether."

"Then we'll just have to help you down to the bus," said Rissa. "That *Emma*'s hardly even conscious any more, and you can't expect to drive all the way down to Westling in the cake van."

"But what about my *cakes*?" cried the baker, wringing his hands. "A small fortune's worth – all spoilt, all smashed – and what about the mess in my van?"

"Oh dear!" Tamzin looked from Jim to Rissa. No one had thought of the money side of the affair.

Old Jim squared his navy-guernseyed cream-plastered chest. "And what if I sues *you*, me lad, for leaving your great pantechnion bang whur I should ram into 'er wid me ole bike? What can a man do when his brakes has gone bust? Well, I tellee – he carsn't heave-to, nor navigate no-how."

"You shouldn't be on the road with an unworthy vehicle," shouted the baker, slipping on a dropped éclair as he swung round to point accusingly at Jim's bike.

"You stove her in!" roared the ferryman. "You scuppered my *Emma* unprovocated, you bottle-nosed, string-gutted saw-fish!"

"If you don't come now, Jim, I'm going to ring for an ambulance," Rissa said loudly and determinedly.

"What – on me one leg?" the old man demanded.

"You can lean on Tamzin and me – or even sit on one of our bikes and we'll push you. The bus goes in ten minutes and there isn't another for two hours."

"But my cakes——" began the baker again, nearly fainting at the desolate sight that was revealed in his van when Jim tottered to his feet.

"Something will be done about them," promised Rissa, "but not now. This is the Westling ferryman and she's the vicar's daughter, so you can easily keep track of everybody."

"We're awfully sorry about them, really we are," Tamzin said apologetically. "And I'm sure Mr Decks is, too."

The ferryman made an explosive noise, but Rissa firmly took his arm.

"What about the *Emma*?" he demanded stubbornly, but found himself being hustled, limping heavily through the crowd.

"She can go in Rissa's garden shed, when we come back for our own bikes," Tamzin said, "after we've seen you on to the bus."

"It looks to me," said Rissa, "as if poor *Emma*'s passed away – and a good thing, too, Jim, if you ask me."

The old man stuck his beard out, as best he could while floundering lamely down the knobbly cobbles, propped on each side by a hustling, determined girl. "She may've bin wrecked as often as what she bin afloat," he said stiffly, "but she bin a good vessel, and cor, darn it, I gotta git about. I going to mend her, see, that's what. Cor! Ay, oh, jumping gin bottles, my blessed leg's all bent to blazes. I lay I'll die of it, too, at my time of life."

"Don't be silly, Jim," said Rissa sensibly. "Sailors don't die of pitching into cake-vans. And I'm sure you can walk faster than this, too."

"Anyway, if you don't we'll only end by having to run," said Tamzin, hurrying him on.

CHAPTER 2

A Crowd of Rescuers

Paradoxically, there were far more people in charge of Westling ferry on the day after Jim's accident than before it. The ferryman's grown-up only son was supposed to be in charge, but when Tamzin rushed round after breakfast and her house-chores to see how Jim was, and found Jimmy strenuously dividing his time between renewing blocks and tackle aboard his fishing smack *Stormy Petrel* and running the ferry, she offered to take over. Roger and Meryon arrived about ten minutes later, having bicycled from Winklesea, and Rissa was there soon after them, so that anyone wanting to be rowed across the river could have chosen his pilot from among four different people.

"We'll take it in order of ages," Meryon said. "I'm the eldest, so I'll take the first lot over, then Rissa, then Roger, then Tamzin – who's taken one lot already, so it works out all right."

"If I'd known we were ferrying I'd have put shorts on instead of jeans," said Roger. He was a cousin of Rissa's but not at all like her. On the surface, everything that Roger was, Rissa was more so. She was more headstrong, more practical and more cheerful. She was three months older and two inches taller, and her hair was much darker and thicker. But under the surface Roger was both more reasonable and more tough. Usually he lived in Hastings, where he and Meryon went to school, but for this month and July his family were renting a furnished house which they thought of eventually buying, not far from Meryon's house in Winklesea. Roger sat on the end of old Jim's bench and began rolling his jeans up. "Your mother told us about the *Emma* ramming a cake-van."

"She's laid up in our shed, now," grinned Rissa, "and Jim's laid up in the 'Conqueror'. Of course, I don't suppose he's allowed to drink except in the proper hours, but Mrs Gudgeon doesn't mind him sitting there, and I expect he finds it nicer than at home with 'Stacia."

"I bet he does," said Meryon dryly. "Funny business, old Jim marrying 'Stacia. I wonder what she was like when they were young?"

"Perhaps old Jim came back from years and years at sea and just married the first girl he saw," suggested Tamzin.

Meryon smiled lazily; his brilliant blue eyes, that were such a strange contrast to his rough black hair, vanished almost completely. "She must have brought on all her guns, and Jim's defences were low because of all those years at sea. How is he, Tamzin? Really groggy, or just having a wonderful time putting it on?"

Tamzin was watching a small party of people approaching the Dunsmere side of the river, along a path that crossed the sand dunes. "I don't think anybody really knows. He won't let anyone look at his leg – you know what he is – but it can't be broken because Rissa and I saw him stand on it, once, and he walked on it when we helped him to the bus."

"The news is practically all over Sussex already," said Roger. "At least, several people we passed, coming down, asked us how he was, but we didn't even know he'd had an accident."

"Customers," said Rissa, looking at the approaching party. "Yours, Meryon."

"Jimmy left us some money for giving change," said Tamzin, "here it is."

No one discussed the affair of Jim and the cake-van while Meryon was rowing across the river, but everyone was thinking about it, so that when Meryon returned, handed out his passengers and beached the boat, it was the first thing that anybody mentioned.

"There must've been an awful mess," said Roger. "I'd like to've seen it," he added wistfully. "It must have been a sight in a lifetime."

"It's really that that worries me," said Tamzin, "the mess, I mean. Somebody's got to pay for it – all those cakes."

"They were Henzie's cakes, too," said Rissa, "quite likely the most expensive in Sussex; but luckily the van wasn't really full."

"Jim never saves," said Meryon. "Not that it would be very easy to, with ferrying. There's a terrible lot of work for a very little money."

"He'd absolutely hate going to prison," said Tamzin. She was staring at the sunlit masts in the little harbour, and the slow, shining river and the windy sky that old Jim must love so much underneath the hard shell of his exterior. Imagining him in prison was like thinking of a falcon in a cage.

"And you can't very well fine a person for owing money," said Roger.

"If only we could——" began Tamzin suddenly.

"I know what you're going to say!" said Meryon,

grinning at her: "'if only we could think of some way of raising the money.' There's practically never been a time in your life when you haven't been trying to raise money for someone or something. It gets progressively more difficult, I suppose, because you must have used up nearly all the ways there are, by now."

Tamzin looked at him carefully, unsure how much he was teasing her and how much taking her seriously, but Meryon said, "Of course we've got to save old Jim. Naturally. Though he'll probably be furious. The thing is, how?"

For some time the four of them made patterns in the shingle with their heels, or stared down the river, or gazed up the Hard for possible customers, or twiddled string for the piebald ferry cat, Billingham.

"We've tried rabbits, and home-made sweets and cakes, and flag-days, and jumble," said Tamzin. "There doesn't seem to be anything else that's really original. Of course we could do one of those things again, but people always seem to take better to something new."

"You're a defeatist," said Meryon, "that's what – listing all the things we have done, and none of the things we *haven't*."

"All right, you list a few to me."

"Well – we haven't given a concert."

Everyone stared at him, and then suddenly four very brisk and cheerful artists came cycling down the Hard with folding stools and knapsacks on their backs, and Rissa insisted on taking her proper turn rowing them over. For the next few minutes everyone was rather busy helping to stack bicycles and get the artists properly aboard, and Rissa took fifteen minutes to row them across the tide-swelling river and bring back the district nurse who had auspiciously arrived at the Dunsmere side just in time.

"And by now, I suppose," said Meryon as Rissa dropped down on to the bench again, counting her money, "everyone's thought of a reason for not being able to do a concert."

"Of course," said Roger. "We haven't the charm, the talent, the fame, or the numbers."

"Except for old Meryon," said Rissa. "He could give an acrobatic display, all right. But imagine the rest of the programme! Tamzin Grey, solo; Roger Lambert, solo; Clarissa Birnie, solo——oh, and Dicky would want to be in it; Dickon Grey, solo. I bet it'd sound like the Last Trump, or Mary Call the Cattle Home, and everyone'd go out."

"Everybody's got *some* talent," insisted Meryon. "There's Roger's mouth organ, and – and——oh well, perhaps no concert, then. All right, what about a Citizens' Advice Bureau? One half of this village never seems to know *properly* what's going on in the other. Think of all the awful rumours that are always flying about."

Tamzin grinned. "Mrs Briggs says you've only got to have a headache at one end of the village to find you're dead before you've reached the other."

"Well, there you are," said Meryon. "We'll make it our job to find out the truth about all local matters and pass it on for a fairly small sum."

"Not too small," said Tamzin.

"Lambert, Birnie, Grey and Fairbrass, Limited," announced Meryon. "Do you require any gossip? We have it all. Ask us if you want to know about Mrs Briggs's bunions, Smiling Morn's prices, local tides, Jim Deck's leg, births, marriages or deaths. If we don't know it, we can find it out. Lowest possible prices, absolute satisfaction guaranteed or goods returnable."

"A lot of people did ask us about old Jim's leg," said Roger.

"It would be fun," sighed Tamzin. "I mean, racing about collecting news and all that. But no one would take us seriously. And no one would dream of *paying* for gossip in a village where it's simply buzzing in the air. Especially as there wouldn't be anything solid to show for it. People do like to *have* things for their money."

"We could write it down on a piece of paper for them perhaps," said Roger, "so that they could have something to take away. We could – oh, hey, I wonder if we could possibly——" but suddenly the ferry became so busy, at both sides of the river, that he never did finish his sentence but jumped up saying instead, "It's my turn; oh, help, look at all those Lillycrop children, and without their mother, too. Are they still all half-fare? And how much do we charge for dogs?"

And then, halfway across the ferry, in a very loaded boat, the Lillycrop dogs started fighting and Hydrangea (an anxious child of six, who was midway in age among the ten incredibly named Lillycrop children) fell into the river in her fright. Without thinking, Roger immediately thrust the oars into the hands of Minerva, who at eleven was the eldest, and dived over the side. But so did ten-year-old Ur Lillycrop, and both the dogs, and so did Meryon in all his clothes except his sweater from the edge of the ferry gangway.

Minerva was not a very seamanlike child, having spent the sad childhood of one who is the eldest of ten and therefore second mother to all of them. When Tamzin and Rissa saw that she was losing headway against the flowing tide they raced off down to the river's edge where various small boats were always tied up; but young Jimmy had also seen the mishap and was approaching with strong sweeping strokes downriver from the *Stormy Petrel*, sculling his tarry dinghy over the stern. By the time Tamzin and Rissa got there, the river was much more crowded with rescuers than with those in distress, in spite of the fact that Wistaria (who was nine) had also fallen in as she was helping Roger and Ur to push and haul Hydrangea back over the side again.

"I lay you better all git back whur you started from, ole young 'uns," said Jimmy when the rescue was completed. He was standing in the stern of his dinghy skilfully moving his single oar just enough to keep stationary as the tide slid past him upstream, in case he might be wanted again.

Roger had clambered aboard, the water sluicing off him, and now sat squelchily down to his oars, reassuring the howling Ariadne (who was only three) as he did so. And then, his black hair streaming down his face as he swam up to the ferryboat, Meryon heaved the smallest dog back among his family, and the dog shook himself as all dogs do and everyone was showered with river water. Hydrangea broke out into loud fresh wailings, though not even a cloudburst could have made her any wetter than falling into the river had; and then Ariadne shrieked out that Bob, the biggest dog, was climbing out of the river at the ferry steps on the wrong side.

"I wunt goo home without Bob! I wunt, I *wunt*!" She stamped her small feet on the bottom of the boat, bouncing up and down in a frenzy on the thwart.

"You shut up, our Arry, or I'll spank yer!" said Minerva distractedly, wishing her mother were there, or anybody else except herself. "We gotta get Hy and Wis and Ur back home, or they'll die of pewmonia."

Roger was already turning the ferryboat with long, strong oar-strokes, and Meryon was slowly striking out

21

after it; but the half-dozen or so people who were waiting on the Dunsmere side began shouting about catching a bus, and Ariadne now shrieked so loudly that heads popped out from several boats moored farther up the harbour.

"I say, Rodge!" Tamzin called from the small white dinghy she and Rissa had grabbed, "we'll fetch the Dunsmere party over, and Bob as well. Tell Ariadne. It's a funny thing," she added to Rissa as they headed for the Dunsmere steps, "but that littlest Lillycrop dog is the most ferocious animal in Westling. They only keep him because he won't let anyone touch the children. Old Bob must have thought the wrong side of the river a much better place than being in the same boat with Tich again, though he is three times the size."

"I say," said Rissa, "won't Jim be furious when he hears we've lost all the fares of all those countless Lillycrops?"

"No fear!" said Tamzin, looking over her shoulder to check the position of the steps: "If Mrs Lillycrop meant to get rid of them all for the day she won't change her mind because of a sousing. She'll spank them soundly, dry the ones that need it, and change their clothes and send them all back again. You'll see."

CHAPTER 3

Parish News Only

Mrs Lillycrop did exactly as Tamzin had said she would, but Tamzin had lived at Westling Vicarage since she was three and knew Mrs Lillycrop (and a great many other people, too) very well indeed. A mid-morning lull set in at the ferry while the young Lillycrops were all being spanked and dried and changed. Meryon and Roger were doing almost the same things for themselves at the vicarage, where Mrs Grey had helpfully produced various old gardening garments of the vicar's, and these interesting goings-on had attracted Tamzin's small brother, Dickon, from an earwig hunt behind the woodshed.

"I really do wish I'd been there to see everyone fall in," he said wistfully, handing a large clerical grey sweater to Roger who had been putting a reef in the legs of the vicar's gardening trousers.

"We didn't fall in!" Roger said indignantly, "we dived, and so did Ur."

"You mean, 'so did he'," corrected Dickon.

"I don't, I mean Ur, the same as I said. Wow, I'm absolutely extinguished in these clothes."

"Oh, *Ur*," said Dickon, suddenly understanding. "Why didn't you say so, then."

Roger opened his mouth, looking at Dickon, and then changed his mind and dropped the subject.

"Had a good snail-haul, Dicky?" Meryon asked, pushing back his hair with both hands but not making much impression on its springy, thick wetness.

"It was earwigs," said Dickon. "Are you going, now? Because if so, can I come too, just in case someone else falls in?"

"No," said Meryon firmly, "no one else is going to fall in. But I tell you what; if you come round to the Point at ten to one we'll take you across the river and back; and the tide'll be pretty high, then, so you'll get a really long row."

"Free?" asked Dickon doubtfully.

"Certainly," said Meryon, "but no earwigs."

"Shall we take these wet things and hang them in the garden?" Roger asked.

Curiously enough, Roger had quite forgotten what he had been saying when the rush began at the ferry, but Tamzin and Rissa had not. As soon as he and Meryon appeared walking down the shingly path to the ferry-hut Rissa said, "You *do* look a sight. What was it you were saying before all this happened, Roger?"

"Saying?" asked Roger. "Was I?"

"About the Citizens' Advice Bureau," said Tamzin. "Do turn round and sit down or something, Meryon – your back view is exactly like Dad's in that get-up, and it makes me feel odd."

Meryon turned round and grinned and at once looked like a Spanish gipsy, in spite of the vicar's garments.

"Oh yes!" said Roger, suddenly remembering, "oh of *course*, yes! Fancy my forgetting. What I was saying *was*, couldn't we start a newspaper?"

Everyone looked at him.

"What sort of a newspaper?" Tamzin asked doubtfully.

"*The Westling News*," Roger said, "Parish News Only. It ought to go down like anything, if we made it interesting enough."

There was a moment of solemn consideration, because this was a completely new idea, different from anything that any of them had done before.

"Well, this old place is always full of news," Roger went on. "Look at just these last two days. Banner headlines about old Jim and the cake-van, and then at least a column or two about the rumpus in the river."

"Two items don't make a newspaper," said Meryon, "no matter how sensational. What are you going to fill up with? To say nothing of how you are going to print it, and also to sell it."

"Filling up wouldn't be much trouble," Tamzin said tentatively, not wanting to go along with Roger's idea too hurriedly. "We could do the same as the other papers do; bits about the weather, farming, fishing, and news of famous personalities."

"What – in *Westling*?" said Rissa.

"Fame is purely relative," Meryon said in a grown-up way. "Lots of Westling people are famous – in Westling. Old Jim certainly is——"

"People would like to read about how his leg was getting on," Roger said.

"And so is Hookey Galley – in an infamous sort of way – and Smiling Morn, and the vicar; and everybody's interested in what the fishing fleet does."

"We do even have properly famous people here on holiday, sometimes," said Tamzin, "or for a day's sailing."

"Then what about competitions?" Roger said.

"Recipes," said Rissa.

"Photographs," said Tamzin.

"It would be wonderful if we could have one of those Agony Aunt columns!" said Meryon. "Do you think people would really write and ask us about their pimples, or what to do about blushing and which of two girls should they marry?"

"I shouldn't think so," said Rissa, snorting with laughter, "but we could make up lovely bits ourselves and put them in as 'signed, Cautious Connie', or 'A Lonely Violet'. They'd put the sales up like anything, I expect, because everyone would be trying to guess who wrote them."

"All this is all very well," said Meryon, coming suddenly back to the facts, "but how are we *really* going to pay for old Jim's cakes? That is, if we actually mean to try."

"Well honestly!" said Roger, "just after I've suggested the best idea we've had for years, and we'd almost worked out how to do it."

Meryon looked at him and the others in mild surprise. "Were we being serious?"

"I don't think most of us were to start with," Tamzin said, "but it did begin to seem rather a good idea as we went on. I don't see why we shouldn't have a go."

"Well, have you thought of all the difficulties?" said Meryon, "or even one? News doesn't just *come*; you have to have reporters to go and look for it. Then it has to be got down on paper – and in enough copies to sell to all the people we'd have to persuade to buy it. It has to be delivered, too – and all this bang in the middle of term when we've got homework nearly every evening."

Tamzin was staring down the river in a preoccupied way at a heraldic cormorant on a solitary post. She suddenly said, "Really, I think things are much more interesting if

26

they're difficult."

"There are four of us," said Roger.

"And the evenings are light till bedtime," said Rissa.

"Rissa and I often do a lot of our homework in the dinner hour," Tamzin said, "and there isn't much work to do with the ponies, either, at this time of the year, with Banner and Cascade at grass all the time, and the same with Rissa's Siani."

"All right," said Meryon, "suppose we've got – or can make – the time – what about printing? I don't think it would be worth doing at all unless we can get orders for at least twelve copies a week. It would have to be a weekly, of course; daily would be quite impossible and monthly wouldn't raise enough money. Well, how are we going to produce the twelve copies? – and more if we get more orders?"

"There's always Dad's typewriter," Tamzin said doubtfully, "but I'm not absolutely sure he'd let us use it; and anyway, I think I can really write quicker than I can type."

"Typing's easier to read than writing – than *my* writing, at least," said Roger.

"Four people writing out twelve copies would only be three each," said Tamzin.

"It would be worse than five hundred lines at school," said Rissa. "And think of having it facing you every week."

"It wouldn't be *half* as bad," said Roger emphatically. "I'd a lot sooner write out pages and pages of interesting Westling news than 'I must not make paper pellets in class' even only one hundred times."

"You can use carbon paper with a typewriter," Rissa said. "That would be three or four copies at once."

"I'll ask Dad about it at lunch time," Tamzin said, "but I only use two fingers and often make awful mistakes –

27

especially with the Y and T, because they're so close together."

"Idiot," said Rissa, "*all* the letters are close to at least one other letter."

"I know, but it's worse with Y and T," said Tamzin. "And often I hit the key that says ⅝ when I mean the back-spacer."

"Never mind, people will just have to put up with little things like that," said Roger. "After all, it isn't every village that's *got* its own newspaper, and it's for a very good cause."

"But we can't say anything about its being for a good cause – at least, not *which* cause," Tamzin said, "because everyone else would probably start to think at once that they were just as good causes themselves as old Jim, and not buy the paper."

"Some people downright disapprove of Jim," said Rissa, "you know what it was like those times when he was smuggling, and things like that."

"We can say it's a non-profit-making concern," suggested Roger.

"How are we going to buy the blank paper to make a start?" Meryon asked. "All businesses need capital for getting started: that's why so few people are their own boss, I expect."

"Surely our combined pocket money for one week would be enough?" said Tamzin. "We could pay ourselves back out of the first sales, and sales after that ought to cover the cost of more paper."

"All my pocket money for this week has gone already," Rissa said, "though it is only Saturday still. I bought a film for my camera on my way down."

"If you bought it from Mr Bridger he'd take it back, if

you haven't opened it," Tamzin said. "One more week
without a film wouldn't matter, would it, compared with
getting the paper started?"

"Oh, well——" said Rissa doubtfully.

"Hell's bells, look at all this lot coming round Smiling
Morn's corner!" said Roger suddenly. He had almost
forgotten that they were in charge of Westling ferry.

"It's the Lillycrops again, just as I said," grinned
Tamzin, looking up from her sandal-doodling in the
shingle. "And more than last time! They've got Cleopatra
with them now, and that's the lot, except for those very
new twins."

"I think we'd better take them in two trips," said
Meryon dryly, "dogs first and Lillycrops after! Anyway,
stand-by, all first-aid stations; and let's hope no one falls in
this time, or we shall have wickedly deceived Dickon."

CHAPTER 4

A Bit of a Secret

Dickon came round to the Point at a quarter to one, asking anxiously whether anyone else had fallen in, and parking his box of earwigs on the end of the bench.

"I said *no* earwigs," Meryon reminded him sternly.

"Oh dear, I quite forgot," explained Dickon. "They won't mind not going across the ferry, of course, but I did think it would be rather *nice* for them to go, because they would find quite different other earwigs over the river."

"I see," said Meryon, "improving the strain on the other side. Well, I don't see that it matters, as long as you don't improve the strain on this side."

"And if he doesn't let them loose in Jim's boat," said Tamzin.

"Or go overboard after them if *they* fall in," said Rissa.

"It's a fairly strong box," Dickon said, putting his thumb over the weakest place in it.

"Well, come along, then," said Tamzin, turning down towards the river. "What a shame there aren't any other customers. It's rather a wasted journey."

It may have been wasted, as Tamzin said, but it was not entirely without excitement, because when Dickon had stumped up the concrete steps on the Dunsmere side and squatted down to open his earwig box he let out a cry of anguished despair. Tamzin dashed up the steps expecting to find him in the grip of at least one earwig's pincers, but he was standing staring bleakly into his empty box.

"What's the matter, Dicky?"

"I've lost my beetle, that was in with the earwigs for company! I *know* he was there at the ferry hut, because I peeped through the crack in the lid, but now he isn't." The small boy's lower lip trembled pathetically. For some reason this was the one thing that Tamzin simply couldn't bear – when Dickon's lip trembled she would have done anything to help him and make him smile again.

"Oh, Dicky!" Her arm was round his hunched shoulders. "Perhaps we can help you find him. Are you sure you didn't let him out here, with the earwigs?" She was gazing into the short, wind-bitten grasses at their feet, but not even seeing any earwigs.

"No, I couldn't have, could I, if he wasn't in the box? He was such a beautiful beetle, too, and I was training him to answer to his name."

"Perhaps he's in the boat, or under the bench at the ferry hut," Tamzin suggested, taking Dickon's hand. "We've still got time for a quick look before lunch."

"Was it a black beetle?" Roger asked from the ferryboat, waiting at the steps.

"N-no," said Dickon, sniffing sorrowfully. "Much more beautifuller than that. I wouldn't have *minded* so much about a black beetle, but Jerusalem was goldy – you know that hymn, Tamzin, 'Jerusalem, the golden'? We had it last Sunday morning, and so——"

"But *are* there any golden beetles?" Rissa asked, looking under the thwarts with interest.

"Well, he wasn't *all* golden," Dickon said grudgingly,

unwilling to diminish the glory of his lost capture, "but he was covered with mag*nifi*cent gold stripes – like a zebra, you know, only they all went one way, down his back——"

Meryon was just pushing off the boat again but now he turned round, letting her drift with the slowing tide, and stared at Dickon with a sudden concentrated interest. "Gold stripes, did you say? Were they black and gold? And how big was the beetle?"

"About as big as that," said Dickon, holding his finger and thumb half an inch apart.

"Dicky, where did you find it? In the potatoes?" Meryon was automatically pulling the ferryboat round to her course.

Looking up from his perusal of the bottom boards Dickon stared at him in astonishment. "Yes, on the leaves. But how did you know?"

"Roaring rum runners!" said Meryon in a low, impressed voice. "D'you know what that probably was?" He looked from one to another of the puzzled boat-load. "A Colorado beetle."

"Oh – one of those things," said Tamzin, finding the name vaguely familiar but not being sure what, if anything, she had ever heard about it.

Rissa fished up a fact from her practical mind. "They live on potato leaves."

"Oh, they're those things people are supposed to look out for!" said Roger, suddenly remembering, "because they're a pest in some countries, aren't they, but not in Britain yet."

"I *am* looking out for him," said Dickon sadly, "but no one else is, very much. He must be either in this boat or somewhere round the ferry hut, because those are the only places I've had him in."

"I don't think he's in the boat," Roger said. "And we'd have a terrible job to find him round the ferry hut – a goldy beetle on goldy pebbles. And anyway, stripes are the most camouflaging thing – that's why zebras and tigers have them, so that they can't be seen in the jungle."

"Never mind, Dicky darling!" Tamzin said, trying to comfort him. "I expect there are lots of other even more beautiful beetles."

"But the thing nobody else seems to have thought of," said Meryon, "is the reward. Isn't there quite a big reward for Colorado beetles?"

"Hey, is there really?" said Tamzin. "I wonder if there are any more beetles on the same potatoes. . . ."

"Think if we could find a dozen or so," said Roger, renewing his search under the duckboards.

"Jerusalem was the only one," said Dickon heavily. "I looked and looked, because I thought he would be lonely by himself. That's why I put him with the earwigs."

"We'll have a really thorough hunt as soon as we land," said Rissa purposefully.

Meryon turned round to see where he was nosing in at the ferry landing and caught sight of Mrs Grey waving a handkerchief from the vicarage balcony over the porch. "We can't," he said. "We're a bit late for lunch already. And when Mrs Grey is nice enough to have the lot of us, the least we can do is not to keep her and Mr Grey waiting."

"Oh, but the reward!" said Tamzin. "I'm sure Mother would understand – just for five more minutes. One of us could go along and tell her."

"Young Jimmy is rowing across from the *Stormy Petrel*," said Roger, climbing out and pulling the dinghy in to the shore. "I expect he thinks we're ready to hand over to him."

"Listen!" said Meryon suddenly, shipping his oars, "we mustn't mention the Colorado to anyone at all, or we'll have everyone else in the village looking for it. At least, say nothing until we find it. Who's going ahead to the vicarage?"

"Dicky, you would, wouldn't you?" Tamzin asked, jumping ashore.

"Oh, *no*! It's my beetle, after all." He was already running sturdily up to the ferry hut.

"I will," Roger offered, "and then I can see if my clothes are dry and change back again before lunch. I feel as if I'd shrunk, or something, in these." He pulled the grey sweater out in front of him, folding it over. "This year's masculine fashion-note – sweaters are being worn double-breasted. . . ."

"Hurry *up*, Roger," said Rissa, "and – oh, oughtn't one of us to hold off Jimmy for a minute or two? Look, Tamzin, you've got the Ferry money, you go down and hand it over when he comes ashore, and ask him how Jim is, and all that. . . . Now, Dicky, where d'you think it might have got out?"

"I know where it might have got *out*, all right," said Dickon, who was somewhere under the long bench, "but what really matters is where he might have got *to*."

"Lost something, then?" young Jimmy asked Tamzin as she counted out the money into his hand. Tamzin glanced hastily over her shoulder.

"Oh, I think Dickon did drop something. . . . How's your father getting on, Jimmy? We haven't seen him this morning."

"Ar. Well. I dunno, rightly, Miss. He wunt let anyone have a look-see, but he don't seem able to walk proper like, and I wholly don't like that. Our Mum, she's trying to get him to go to the surgery, and mebbe he might do that if his leg don't clear up nacheral."

"Oh dear," said Tamzin, "I wish he would. . . . Tell him we asked after him, won't you?"

"I will that, but I lay you might see him, prenly. He's threatening for to git back ferrying, see. He say you don't need two legs for rowing. Stubborn, ent he?"

"Well, I suppose he always was, really," said Tamzin, wondering how the searchers were getting on, and how long she could keep young Jimmy talking.

Back at the ferry hut Meryon was carefully lifting a heap of nets. "If only we could find the darned thing we mightn't need to start the newspaper at all – if I'm right about the reward."

"What newspaper?" asked Dickon abstractedly, from behind a pile of lobster-pots.

"Oh, but I think it might be *fun* to run the paper," said Rissa, who was on her hands and knees gently combing her fingers through the shingle. "Do look where you're putting your great beetle-crushers."

"First time I've ever thought that expression apt," said Meryon. "Oh bother! Here's Jimmy coming up already. I suppose we can always offer to do the ferrying again this afternoon, but I had thought we might have done a bit of preliminary reporting."

Meryon and Rissa and Dickon immediately began trying to look as though they really hadn't been hunting for anything at all, but Jimmy both knew that they had and knew perfectly well they were pretending that they hadn't.

"Lost something?" he inquired again, striding slowly up to the hut with Tamzin walking anxiously beside him.

"Oh, er, nothing much," said Rissa carefully. "Just

35

something one of us dropped."

"Well, if you let me know what it were," said Jimmy, "I'll know if I find it, wunt I?" He was glancing around on the shingle for anything that might be unusual there.

"Really," said Dickon, "it's mine. I dropped it, and it's about *so* big, Jimmy, and all goldy-stripy coloured – Rissa, you're standing on my foot!"

"Ah, a sort of brooch, or charm, or summat, eh?" said Jimmy, comprehending.

"We simply must rush now," said Meryon, "but – well actually, it's a bit of a secret in a way. I mean, it might be terribly unlucky for us to mention exactly what it is, you see. Would you like us to come round again for a bit, this afternoon? We really don't mind if it's any help."

"It would keep old Dad orf his feet for a while," said Jimmy gratefully. And then, "Funny thing about charms. I had an uncle once what kept an Egyptian charm. Shaped like a beetle it were. He called it a scarab, and said it were terrible unlucky to speak of it by name, so he allus wrote it down if anybody asked."

There was a moment's awkward silence in which everybody hoped that Jimmy would not suddenly produce a pencil and paper, but he only said cheerily, "Well, I'll keep a look-out and let you know if I find anything. See you later, then," and strode off over the shingle to fetch old Jim from the "William the Conqueror" and help him home.

CHAPTER 5

Damages Being Dealt With

At lunch, which was in the vicarage garden because the June day was warm and sunlit, the vicar astonished everyone by announcing that not only had he persuaded Jim Decks to let a doctor see him, but that the doctor had already done so and prescribed treatment.

"But well, goodness, sir," said Roger, "I thought Jim was in 'The Conqueror' all the morning. We never saw him come out, did we, Tamzin? It just shows how elusive the old bloke is."

"As it happens," said the vicar, "the doctor was in the 'Conqueror', too, and so was I. And as presumably none of you saw us go in – or come out, either – it just shows how unobservant you all are."

"I expect we were busy with the ferry," said Tamzin.

"You were all sitting on the bench outside the ferry hut staring absently into space," said the vicar. "Some more corned beef to finish up your lettuce, Rissa? There's plenty here."

Tamzin was balancing her plate on her knee in the awkward manner of deckchair diners, and fending off Willow and Schnooky, the vicarage cats. "What did Doctor Hargreaves say? – I suppose that's who it was."

The vicar dropped a slice of corned beef on to Rissa's plate and another on to his own and sat back blinking in the sun. "Well, first, he said would Jim join us in a drink, and then we all got talking about boats, and that led to fishing and so by devious routes to smuggling: and after that Hargreaves could have taken Jim's appendix out there and then without too much opposition."

"Wow!" said Roger again, very much impressed.

"Anyway, he soon had Jim pulling off his seaboot and rolling up his trouser-leg, just where he was in the bar-parlour. The old chap was rather proud of it, I think, pointing out what an awful purple colour it was going, and——"

"Richard, dear, we're having lunch," his wife said reprovingly.

"Sorry, Gwen," the vicar smiled in the abashed way of an admonished but well-loved small boy. "Anyway, it seems Jim hasn't really damaged himself very much – nothing broken, I mean; but it's a bad sprain, with a muscle pulled and probably torn a little, and he's got to keep off it for a week or two, possibly longer."

"I bet he was furious about that," said Tamzin, hoping no one had noticed the shred of corned beef that she had just dropped – against vicarage rules – into ginger Schnooky's mouth.

"He was, of course," said the vicar. "He said he simply wouldn't do it – he was going to run the ferry and dash about as usual. But the doctor and I suddenly remembered that invalid carriage that Mrs Biddle left him in her will for the use of any needy Dunsford patient. He hasn't got any takers at the moment, it seems: all the Dunsford folk are in a state of quite astonishing mobility; so he offered to lend it to Jim."

Mrs Grey, with one eye on young Dickon who was offering a piece of lettuce to an unsuitably approaching snail, shook her head and said wisely, "Jim would simply hate that. I couldn't imagine him ever taking to an invalid chair. He'd rather die in his boots."

"That's exactly what he's often said," Tamzin remarked. "About his boots, I mean."

"He'd feel he was really getting old," said Roger sadly. "Poor Jim."

"Well, you're terribly wrong," said the vicar, twinkling round at them all. "He was thrilled. Mrs Biddle's invalid carriage isn't a bath-chair, you know; it's a little motor vehicle. They can go quite fast on a good road, can't they, Meryon?"

"Well, how would I know?" said Meryon, grinning widely. "So he's going to scorch up and down the Marsh and imperil all the villagers, is he?"

"This'll be worse than his sailing bicycle was," said Mrs Grey, reminiscing, "though that was dangerous enough."

"Does he have to have an L-plate?" Rissa asked.

"Of course," said Roger.

"It looks as if we're going to have some things to report in our paper, anyway," Tamzin said.

"What paper?" said Dickon, turning round from his snail. "You said about a paper at the ferry."

"Oh, yes," said Tamzin, "Dad, d'you think we could possibly use your typewriter fairly often, if we're really careful? We're going to start publishing a paper."

Her father looked at her carefuly. "A paper. Supposing you tell me something about it."

Everyone told him about it at once, and Mrs Grey hesitated before taking the trolley back into the house for the pudding until she heard the gist of it, too.

"Could I be a reporter?" Dickon asked. "I know lots of things about the village that all of you don't, because I know differenter people than you do."

"Our reporters don't get any wages, of course," Meryon said, "but all voluntary contributions will be considered."

"What did you say?" asked Dickon, puzzled, but Meryon was now trying to listen to Tamzin and her father discussing the typewriter.

"I don't mind your using it, if you really are careful," the vicar was saying, "but I'm not sure that I agree with the cause you're working for. Quite likely Jim has any amount of money tucked away somewhere, though he'd never admit it; but in any case he's rather a headstrong old tough, and I dare say it would do him good to have to pay for his own damages."

"But, Dad, in a sense it was all my fault. He was waving to me at the top of the hill, and it was that that made his bicycle get out of control. He would never have seen me at all if I hadn't shouted."

Mr Grey knew of old how dogged Tamzin could be when she felt that her loyalty and honour were in question.

"I see. Though I don't think I agree with you, since you only shouted in friendliness. I should say the trouble was in the unroadworthiness of Jim's bike. However, if you feel you want to help in paying for the cakes I wouldn't dream of stopping you. You've thought of the problems of fitting it all in with school and homework, I suppose?"

"We thought we could do it, sir," Meryon said. "At least, we thought we'd have a try. It may only be a smallish newsheet, until term ends; we'll have to see how things work out."

"Unless we find Dicky's beetle," said Rissa.

"Beetle?" asked Mrs Grey, who had now returned with a

large bowl of apple fluff, and again everyone began to explain. Mr Grey at once started bolting his fluff out of anxiety for his potatoes and hurriedly strode off to look at them for more signs of the dangerous invader, although Dickon swore that there couldn't be another after the search he had made himself of every single leaf.

"It was his favourite pudding, too," said Mrs Grey. "I don't suppose he even tasted it."

"If anyone *does* find my beetle," said Dickon suddenly, stopping scraping his plate to say it, "he's still *my* beetle, for me to sell or keep if I want to. And if I sell him it's really my money – isn't it, Mother?"

"Oh, but Dicky!" said Tamzin. "Surely it isn't still his if he loses it, Mother, and someone else finds it?"

Mrs Grey tried not to look as baffled as she felt about this question. "Well, if you lost Cascade, and Minerva Lillycrop found him——" she began, but Tamzin cried out, "Oh, but Mother, beetles are *different*. Aren't they, Meryon? Nobody ever really owns them, the way they do horses."

"So then you can't own Jerusalem, any more than I can, if you do find him," said Dickon.

"Much better not to argue until he is found," suggested Meryon, making peace.

"I'm going round to look for him now – may I, Mother?" Dickon asked, jumping up with his empty plate.

"When you've helped to carry something indoors," said his mother, gathering up the spoons.

"And don't do it too obviously," Roger reminded him, "or you'll have the whole village round there hunting for him too."

Meryon took the spoons from Mrs Grey's hands and firmly settled her back in her chair again, placing the morning paper on her lap. "You stay where you are in the sun for a bit, and we'll do the dishes. It won't take four of us any time, and after all you did the cooking."

Tamzin nearly said, "I did do the breakfast ones," but was ashamed of the thought before it could express itself and began swiftly collecting plates and glasses.

They made a human chain in the scullery. Meryon, wrapped in Mrs Grey's frilly apron, did the washing up, Tamzin sorted the things from the rinsing basin, putting some in the rack and passing some back to Roger for drying, and Rissa put everything away.

"But just fancy Dickon turning out so awkward over the beetle," Tamzin was saying sadly, passing the salad bowl back to Roger.

"I suppose that's the worst of having a small brother," Rissa said, which started Tamzin defensively saying that Dickon wasn't usually like that, and Meryon intervened for peace again in the way he generally did.

"It is his beetle, after all, and probably no one will ever see it again anyway. We'd better forget it and push on with the paper. Half of us could make a start this afternoon; it doesn't take four to run the ferry."

"What about working in two shifts," suggested Roger, looking at his face in a spoon he had just dried. "Two reporters and two ferrymen, swapping over after an hour or so."

"We ought to have notebooks," Rissa said, "and pencils, of course."

"I've got one fairly new notebook," said Tamzin. "The reporters'll have to share it. I'm afraid some of the pages are already full of horses' names and a birthday list and drawings and books I want to read, but lots of them are blank."

"Which of us is doing what?" Roger asked. "Really, I think Tamzin ought to be in the first shift of reporters because it's her village and she knows it best."

"Well, if I am, I'd like Meryon to come with me, because he's wonderful with old ladies," Tamzin said. "They always tell him everything, whether he asks them or not."

"Then that's not a fair division," Rissa objected, "the best two together. If Tamzin's in the first lot, Meryon ought to be in the second. Where do the salad servers go, Tamzin?"

"In the kitchen table drawer – and this is the last thing to dry. All right, who shall I take?"

"Me," said Roger, with his hand on his breast and a seraphic smile.

"I .don't mind," said Tamzin. "Hurry up, then, it's already five to two. And do comb your hair. We've got to make a really good impression."

"Er – do we know what our paper is called?" said Meryon, who was mopping out the sink. "Or what it costs? Or when it comes out?"

Tamzin paused in her flight through the doorway to get her notebook. "Aren't we idiotic? Well, didn't Roger say *The Westling News*? And it could be every Saturday night, and costing – what?"

"Not too expensive for a news-sheet," Rissa said, "or people won't buy it."

"If it's got things about their neighbours in it, they will," said Meryon shrewdly. "It'll have to be at least eighteen pence, and even at that it'll take a terribly long time to pay the damages."

"If only we could sell enough copies it wouldn't," said Tamzin. "We'll all have to try to get orders: you and Meryon while you're ferrying, Rissa. First issue out next

Saturday, anyway."

"Next Saturday as ever is," said Roger.

"And somebody had better tell Mr Henzie that the damages are being dealt with," Rissa said, "so that he doesn't worry Jim."

"We could compose a letter; it would be more business-like," said Meryon.

"And sign it, The Editor, *Westling News*," said Roger.

"I say – who *is* the editor?" Tamzin suddenly asked, whisking round in the doorway again.

"Why, Roger, of course," said Rissa. "He thought of it."

"Oh, I say!" said Roger, grinning broadly. "Fancy me, an editor! Really me?"

"Not anyone," said Tamzin, "if we don't get going now. Oh, help – I nearly forgot my notebook after all. I won't be half a minute . . ."

"Ready, Rissa?" Meryon said, twirling his dishmop and hanging it up. "Help me out of this silly apron, and then it's you and me for the galley. Saturday afternoon – and a fine one – we ought to do a lot of business at the ferry."

CHAPTER 6

Something Very Strange and Rare

"Well, where are we going?" Roger asked as he hurled himself over the vicarage back gate after Tamzin. They paused for a moment on the grass verge, looking at each other.

"Smiling Morn's shop," said Tamzin, suddenly decisive. "A few pence spent there will be well worth it, if only he's in a good mood: all the news gets to the shops or the pubs first."

"He isn't usually very forthcoming," said Roger as they went across the road.

"Even if we only get him grumbling," said Tamzin, "he might grumble some news."

The village stores was opposite the vicarage and very handy. Its two windows were characteristically decorated with packets of detergent and broomheads, a tower of fly-papers – very seasonable – and a column of tins of peas.

"We'll have to take as long a time as we can," whispered Roger as they opened the door, setting off the death-knell clang of the shop-bell.

There was, apparently, no one in the shop, except for a hundred or two droning flies describing their aimless straight lines in the cheese-scented air.

"He must be——" Tamzin began, and then suddenly there rose from behind the counter, like Venus from the waves (or more probably a body from a tomb) the melancholy face of Mr Goldeye, the Westling grocer.

"We thought you were somewhere in the back," explained Tamzin, jingling her coins.

"I was behind the counter," said the grocer in sombre tones, "picking up split peas."

"Oh, how dreadful for you," said Tamzin sympathetically. "Did you drop them, Mr Goldeye?"

"Hole in the bottom of the bag," Mr Goldeye said, smiling sepulchrally and then yanking his face back to normal.

Roger was looking at the sweet department, which consisted of five jars (not much chance of dallying over that), and somewhere in the house at the back of the shop Mrs Goldeye was singing "My Mother Said I Never Should" with her usual extreme and astonishing joviality.

"Toffees, dolly mixtures, bulls' eyes, mint drops, jelly babies," said her husband, slapping his large hands down on the counter like a couple of bare feet, "or is it something for your ma?"

"Couldn't we help you pick up the peas?" Roger offered tentatively. But from the point of view of the *Westling News* this was a mistake, for Smiling Morn at once accepted, saying that he could just nip round to unpack his sultanas while they did so, and would they shout if anyone came in because he didn't always hear the bell and the missus mightn't bother.

"Just look what you've done," said Tamzin. "We've got to pick them up now you've offered."

Roger groaned. "Don't pile it on. D'you think I can't see the lovely headline it makes – 'Hole in Grocer's pea-bag'?"

46

"Well, don't pick them up one at a time, anyway."

Some three minutes later the door-bell suddenly clanged again, by which time Roger and Tamzin were both thoroughly ruffled, having banged each other's heads twice and knelt on split peas three times between them, and not picked up more than half of what was there. Peering up over the counter they beheld the fattest woman in Westling, Mrs Beatup.

"Well, my blessed aunt and all the saints!" said Mrs Beatup, making a gesture that would have been clutching her bosom if that area hadn't been so large, "you had me proper frit."

Mrs Beatup was really rather nice, though Tamzin could never quite forgive her for marking the edges of her pie-crusts with a set of sunday false teeth, as she had once seen her doing ("It makes a lovely pattern, ducks"). She was also an expert gossip, when she wasn't too busy, and remembering this Tamzin rushed in with her story of the paper before the grocer could come back from whatever grocing he was doing out at the back. But unfortunately Mrs Beatup was very busy; she had left her pastry already rolled out on her kitchen table before discovering that she was short of jam for filling it.

"Otherwise, love, I could give you lots of bits for to put in your paper. Look, give me that jar of raspberry, there's a duck, and tell the old corpse when he comes in."

Roger hastily grabbed the jar from the shelf, slipping on the split peas as he did so, and Tamzin took the money, saying, "When we've picked up the rest of these peas, if we shouldn't be a frightful nuisance, we could come up to your house and you could tell us the bits of news you were just mentioning, while you finish your jam tarts."

Mrs Beatup paused halfway to the door, the floorboards

creaking under her. "Well now, you know you're allus welcome, even if it were ever so. But I tell you one thing, now that's *really* new, on account of our Johnny only telled me five minutes ago." She lowered her voice as one imparting a state secret. "There's a real funny bird out at Cloudesley Castle, he say. Proper rare, I wouldn't wonder, like as if it were a sort a bird of paradise. All coloured, and with a hem great crest, he say, what it flipped up and down, and then it went into the wall somewheres, and he never saw it no more."

"I say!" said Roger, "that really is news."

"Well, if it's any use to you, there it is," said Mrs Beatup cheerfully, cramming her twenty stone through the shop doorway, but Tamzin threw herself over the counter and rushed out saying eagerly, "You will order a copy, won't you, Mrs Beatup? It's for a really good cause, and most likely Johnny's name will be in it, and eighteen pence isn't really very much, with prices going up the way they are."

"All right, love, put me down for one then; or look, I'll have three if our Johnny's in it. Gor! what a lark – but mind you put something nice," and she turned her great weight homewards like a motherly brontosaurus to its den.

"As soon as we've picked up these so-and-so peas," said Tamzin, whirling back behind the counter, "we'll get the ponies and tear out to Cloudesley Castle."

"What, me on Banner?" asked Roger dubiously, for he and Meryon had never been the enthusiastic riders that Tamzin and Rissa were, and Dickon's Banner was really too small.

"Of course – unless you'd rather ride Cascade. I don't really mind."

"It isn't which pony, it's the tearing that I mind about."

"All right, then we won't tear very fast, but we've got to

get there and back in much less than an hour. Oh, do try to pick up the wretched things a little bit faster!"

Tamzin and Roger rode down the village street some fifteen minutes later.

"Really, I suppose we ought to have asked Dickon if it was all right our taking Banner," Tamzin was saying, "but he hadn't come back from the ferry hut."

"Still looking for his Colorado," said Roger, settling himself in Banner's saddle and feeling rather foolish to be riding such a small pony; but the Marsh shepherds (lookers, they were called) always rode ponies, and of course the Dartmoor farmers and Welsh hill farmers never rode anything else.

"I wonder if we ought to stop and tell Mrs Beatup we shan't be going to her house until later," Tamzin said uncertainly, and then, "We're awfully short of time, and I expect she'll guess we've gone to look for the bird."

Roger put down a cautious hand to make sure that his stirrups weren't twisted. "Myself, I should have thought the village would be much more interested in a bit of genuine gossip, such as Mrs Beatup could have told us, than in a rare bird."

"It depends how rare," said Tamzin. "I say, I wish I had a pocket-size bird book. We'll just have to make very careful notes and look it up afterwards."

They rode on past Church Cottages, where Mrs Beatup lived, and past the village school, the green and the little church on its waste of tawny shingle, past the Beach Works, noisily churning pebbles inside its great steel gizzards for making concrete, and then they opened a lichen-greened gate and rode out on to the quiet, wide acres of the Marsh. The Beach Works was only a grumble on the south-east wind behind them, now: ahead was the uttermost edge of the world's most famous grazing land, where more sheep were carried to the acre than in any other place.

"I never ride across here," Tamzin was saying, "without thinking how once it was all under the sea."

"The whole of it is still under sea *level*," said Roger, "at high tide. Everyone's lives and land depend on the sea-wall."

"I wonder if there were as many fishes as there are sheep and lambs, now? Don't they look absolutely dazzling, dazzling white, after shearing?"

"Keep your eyes on the castle," said Roger, "in case the bird flies out."

"We were rather stupid," said Tamzin, "not to have asked more about what it looked like. Hey, you don't really mind galloping for a bit, do you? It's a lovely stretch for it, here."

"All right, but don't blame me if I go overboard."

The squat, grey stone castle with its heavy rounded bastions seemed suddenly to come much closer, as they thudded beside the sheep-paths watched by motherly ewes that bleated anxiously for scattered lambs. Floating lightly on the smooth green levels were wind-bent flowering thorn trees, like puffs of spindrift on a calm green sea, and there were redshanks all along the tide-creeks, calling like a carillon of little silver bells.

The ponies' hoofs brushed through a lake of green-gold lady's bedstraw, and the hay-sweet scent blew up in their riders' faces.

"There's no one with the sheep," said Tamzin, drawing back to a very slow canter. "No one at the castle that I can see. No one anywhere at all."

"Which makes us all the more likely to see the bird," said Roger, puffing and bumping at her side.

Slowing to a walk as they came near the castle they began to ride around its bluff outer walls. Now the ponies' hoofs were hidden in a sea of meadow buttercups, and the soft summer wind blew through gully reeds.

A sudden clattering flutter from the broken walls made Tamzin pull in Cascade when they were halfway round, and two large clumsy birds went away on the wind towards Castle Farm, at the farthest edge of the grazings.

"Jackdaws," Roger said. "No headlines in those."

They rode on silently back to their starting point, seeing no more birds but a flight of wild duck very high in the windy sky and a tick-hunting starling on a sheep's back. Pulling in again at the hole in the wall that once had been the castle gateway Roger glanced at Tamzin. "When we ride round inside, I'll watch the outer wall and you watch the middle keep."

Inside the castle five grazing sheep lifted nervous heads and began to trot anxiously ahead of the approaching riders. Here the Marsh had long since moved in, and where once soldiers had tramped and slept and eaten, the short lush grasses of the sheep levels were established.

No one spoke – except for, once, an apprehensive ewe. The only sound was a gentle jingling of bridles, for hoofs made no noise on the velvet of the grass. Roger's eyes scarcely noted the great open fireplaces set in the outer wall because he knew them so well, just as Tamzin hardly saw the crumbling inner stair, all flamed with yellow wallflowers. They were looking, not for what they knew, but for something very strange and rare. Then, suddenly, they saw it. At least, they were absolutely positive that they saw it, but unfortunately neither of them was looking at the place from where it came. Out of the corners of their eyes they both saw a swooping streak of dusky, exotic-looking pink and a flash of boldly barred wings, before it had gone over their heads and out of their sight beyond the top of the circling outer wall.

"Look! Oh, look!" Roger swung little brown Banner on his haunches and went drumming round the tall keep to the gateway.

"Rodge – quick!" Tamzin had set Cascade at the long sweeping slope of grass that rose in green waves on the ancient rubble of fallen stones, almost, in places, to the wall-top. It was very steep, but it was the quickest way to see beyond the wall and Cascade would have had a gallant try at a railway embankment if Tamzin had put him to it.

When Roger had thudded through the gateway and round the grey walls to the seaward side, he pulled up and gazed around him. The only remarkable thing that he saw at all was Tamzin on her shining white pony, looking strangely unreal against the sky, as if she were on a winged horse that had alighted on the wall-top.

"Did you see where it went?" His voice floated up, above the bleating of disorganised sheep.

"No, nothing at all. Did you?"

Roger shook his head. "Perhaps we oughtn't to have ridden into the castle. Or at least we ought to have had one of us outside all the time. But really, scouting on foot would have been better."

"It could be in one of those clumps of willows," Tamzin called. Cascade was pawing with a front hoof and Roger heard the ring of his shoe on stone. "I don't think it could have flown to Castle Farm without our seeing it."

"How much time have we got?"

"Not any, really, if we're going to do our whack at the

ferry, and we promised to do that. We'll be late already. I'll come along down, but keep a lookout."

Cascade swung round, flashing white against the blue of the summer sky, and his tail swirled up like a fountain as he plunged down the slope and out of Roger's sight.

Roger pressed his legs against Banner's sides and trotted round again to the gateway. "Well, anyway," he said as Tamzin rode out of the shadow of the wall, "we have seen the bird, and it did look unusual, didn't it?"

"I think so," said Tamzin, swinging round beside him, "but what are the others going to say? I don't think our innings has been a very strong one on news, somehow, do you?"

"It all takes time," said Roger, bumping along towards the village again. "We may not actually have the news yet, but at least we've found out where the news is. And there's always tomorrow."

CHAPTER 7

Editing and the Literary Life

The first thing Roger and Tamzin saw when they were running down the Hard to the ferry hut was Dickon arranging a few wilting potato leaves as decoys in likely places.

"I've spent all afternoon looking for him," he said sadly, "and then I thought he must be getting hungry, and if he is he'll come tearing out of wherever he is when he sniffs potato leaves, and then I can catch him."

"Oh." Tamzin had rather lost interest in the Colorado since Dickon's sudden refusal to let it help with Jim Decks' cake fund. "Did Daddy say you could have the leaves?"

"Well, he didn't azackerly *say*," said Dickon cautiously. "But then I· didn't azackerly ask. I just said I thought Jerusalem would be missing his leaves, and Daddy said Yes, but I don't *think* he was really listening because it's Saturday and he was swotting up a sermon. Anyway, at least he did say Yes."

"You just wait till he looks at his potato patch, Dicky!" said Roger warningly, and then caught sight of the ferryboat coming into land and old Jim rowing it. "Look at that! And where are the others?"

Tamzin glanced up. "He did say he was going to. Look,

54

he's using a boathook for a stick."

Jim Decks came rolling and swaying up the Hard, half-dragging and half-swinging his injured leg, his little ear-rings flashing gold under the white flash of his hair. "I said I wouldn't lay up, and I ent," he said defensively. "Gorblimey and sink me for a coghead if anyone's gooing to make a ruddy invalid of me – though I will say I wholly fancy that ole motor chair what the doctor say he give me a loanst of. He ent brung it down to the vicarage yet, has he, old young 'uns?" The old man sat down heavily on the end of his bench with his bad leg stuck out stiffly in front of him.

"We haven't been in there since lunch," Roger said.

"Where are the others?" asked Tamzin. "We thought they were ferrying."

Jim Decks picked up his black-and-white cat who was purring her delight at his return. "We-ell, now – 'cept for this young chap what's a-trying to grow spuds in the shingle, seemingly – I dunno. They bin and took off when I took over. Said they got a dunnamany things to do, and dashed off smartish."

"They're in the stable," said Dickon. "I heard them when I was in the potatoes."

"Well, why didn't you say before?" asked Tamzin impatiently. "We'll go and look, Jim. Do be careful with your leg, won't you? And Jim, don't you worry about those cakes, because we've got an idea."

"Dah!" said Jim scornfully. "Don't you worry, neether, gal. I wuzn't a-gooing to be bullied into paying nuthen, choose how; nor nobody else need, I'll lay. Ole Henzie he shouldna left his blessed van whur he did, for me to pitch into, stands to reason."

"But Jim," began Tamzin, and then, thinking better of

launching into an interminable argument with him, waved her hand and dashed after Roger up the Hard.

Meryon and Rissa were in the stable loft, now cleared of its winter hay and swept and bare and roomy.

"Hallo, bring in your news!" called Rissa down the ladder as the stable door creaked and banged. "We've made a terrific start at our end."

"Don't you think this makes a wonderful headquarters?" Meryon asked. "Editor's desk," he indicated a sturdy wooden goat-bench on which a long-forgotten vicarage goat had stood for milking. "Editor has to sit on the floor, of course, but you don't mind that, do you, Rodge? I dare say there's a busted hassock in the church that Mr Grey wouldn't mind you having if you think the floor lacks editorial dignity."

"We had a terrible job getting the bench up," said Rissa. "In the end we hauled it up on the old pulley that used to be meant for bales and things, but as there's no rope we had to borrow the clothes-line from Mrs Briggs."

"She was rather sporting, actually," said Meryon. "She gave us this perfectly good box that Smiling Morn had sent the groceries in: if we have it up on end, like this, it makes a fantastic file. Of course, all this is only if Tamzin likes it; after all, it is her stable."

"I think it's wonderful," said Tamzin. "Much better than trying to find a quiet corner in the house."

"We can even haul up the ladder after us if we simply must have total peace," said Roger, sitting down on a corner of the goat-bench.

"And not only that," Rissa said, "but we've got so much news, and taken so many orders, I don't see why we shouldn't bash the first edition through today, for delivery tomorrow or early Monday morning."

56

"You have?" Roger looked astonished.

"Well, I expect you've got more than we have, of course," said Rissa modestly, "as you've been doing nothing else, and we've had to fit reporting and canvassing in with some ferrying – before Jim sent us packing – and sweeping and furnishing the office."

"Well, really, we haven't got either an awful lot of news or very many orders," said Roger tentatively. It did seem rather an admission of inefficiency and failure.

"How many orders?" Rissa asked. "We've got six: Mrs Gudgeon at the Conqueror – she told us some of our news——Mrs Briggs, of course; the Clenches at the Sailors' Institute; then Onion Ed – he was bringing veg. to the back door when we dashed in——see, that's four, isn't it? Oh, and Doctor Hargreaves – he just brought old Jim's jet-propelled chair——"

"Oh, good," said Tamzin, "he asked about that."

"And your mother, Tamzin," Rissa finished.

"Your father gave us a whole lot of old sermon paper, too," said Meryon, slapping a hand down on the pile stacked neatly in the box, "and he said if the first edition was a really good one he'd order two more in future to send to the grandparents. So with your orders, too, we ought to have quite enough for a start."

"Well, actually, we've only got one order," Tamzin admitted apologetically, "though she said she'd have three if we put Johnny in it, and that was Mrs Beatup, that we saw in Smiling Morn's——"

"Only *one*?" Rissa could hardly believe it. "Didn't you even ask Smiling Morn? Mrs Goldeye would've had one, anyway, I'm sure."

"Well, you see, he wasn't in the shop much, and Mrs Beatup said something that sent us tearing off to Cloudesley Castle straight away, and well, that's how it was, and we've only just got back."

"Hot news out at the castle?" Rissa asked. She was leaning against the weather-boarded wall twiddling a pencil.

Roger swung round to look at her. "Who *is* the editor of this wretched paper?" he demanded, suddenly standing up to his cousin in a way he rarely did. "We couldn't help the news not turning out as hot as we'd expected."

"*One* order and *no* news," said Rissa, but hoping she hadn't gone too far.

"We haven't got the news yet," Tamzin said, "but we know where it is. It's a very rare bird, at the castle. We actually saw it – both of us – but we don't know what it is yet, or if it's nesting or anything."

"What did it look like?" asked Meryon, suddenly interested.

"We hardly saw it for long enough." Tamzin looked at Roger questioningly.

"Well, sort of pinkisk," said Roger.

"And barred somewhere – its wings, I think," said Tamzin, "and about as big as a cuckoo, say. I know I've never seen anything like it before."

"That's not much to go on," said Meryon doubtfully. "I mean, there isn't enough to put in the paper. Not in this edition, anyway, though we could follow it up for another one."

"I don't think it really matters much," Rissa said. "We've got more than enough news for one issue already – though I had hoped Tamzin and Rodge might have brought in a real headliner." She fished a notebook from her jeans pocket and opened it. "We've got the fire in Mrs Smeed's kitchen, and Albert Clench's mammoth cabbage, and

Onion Ed's violin solo that he's practising for, and the measles outbreak at Dunsmere, and Hookey Galley's fight with Walter Goddard."

"It doesn't sound as much as I thought," said Meryon.

"And Hookey's fighting isn't really news at all," said Tamzin, "because he's always fighting someone, some-where, being Westling's most savage and sinister character. What really would be news, now, is Hookey doing anyone a favour. But we can't hope for that."

"We've already got the absolute snip about Jim and the cake-van," Rissa said, making a note in the margin about it.

"And the Lillycrop triple ducking," said Roger with a grin. "I don't see why it shouldn't be enough. If not, surely we can work up some feature items between us? What about the recipe for your mother's apple salad, Tamzin? That really is something, that is."

"I suppose so," said Tamzin, "and we could have a competition, but that would mean a prize, and that would mean expense."

"No, it wouldn't," said Meryon suddenly. "I've still got three appalling handkerchiefs that someone gave me last Christmas and I wouldn't dream of using myself. They're in a box and would make a terrific prize."

"Can't anybody do some verses, or a little story?" Roger asked. "Tamzin, you used to write heaps of poetry. You must have a line or two somewhere."

"Well . . ." said Tamzin dubiously.

"I know the shortest ghost story in the world," said Meryon. "Everybody else probably knows it, too, but it would make a sort of tailpiece."

"Supposing we lay out what we've got in a rough draft," said Rissa in a businesslike voice, "and then brush it up,

59

and then go down to the house and type it."

Tamzin groaned. "That'll be me."

"I can type a bit," Meryon said. "Anyway, I can use four fingers, which is twice as many as you can." He reached for the stack of sermon paper and put it on the goat-bench beside Roger. "The editor is requested perishing well to get down to it."

It took rather a long time to rough out all the material, even with all four of them working on it, and then teatime intervened, so that it was past six o'clock before the typing was begun. The typewriter was set up on the kitchen table because Mr Grey was working at his sermons for the next day in his study and the dining-room table had been newly polished by Mrs Briggs the day before. Meryon carefully fitted in a top-sheet and five carbons and struck the first few words; the paper's name and price and purpose.

"*The Westling News* (Parish News *Only*)

Number One. Price Eighteen Pence. Page One."

"And then the date," said Tamzin. "You'd better put Monday's because Dad doesn't want us to deliver it on Sunday and it won't be ready for tonight."

"Now, first the Editorial," Meryon said, tapping out the word in capital letters. "You dictate it, Rodge – not too fast or I won't guarantee what comes down."

Tamzin and Rissa read it over his shoulder as he typed.

"The purpose of this paper is to give no news that hasn't originated in Westling Parish. All news is as true as we can make it, though we do not hold ourselves responsible for this. We have no intention of competing with any other newspapers, until such time as another paper devotes itself exclusively to Westling news. We wish all our readers well and hope that they will go in for our competitions. The first one is to be found on page——"

"Leave that blank," said Roger, "until we see what page it is on. Next is the bit about Jim. 'Westling Ferryman Dives into Cake-Van'."

Tamzin had written this article because she had the best eyewitness knowledge of the incident, and Meryon got it all down with only two fractions and an asterisk where they shouldn't be. He went on to "Three Young Inhabitants O.B.".

"That stands for overboard, of course," he said. "Everyone in Westling will know."

"Mrs Lillycrop's sure to buy a copy," said Tamzin, "with this bit about Ur's diving after his sisters. What a pity we can't do photographs. I suppose sketches are possible, but we'd have to do a different one for each copy."

"Pin-men drawings would be fairly easy," said Rissa. "We could all do those, and they might look rather good. Leave a space there, Meryon, if Roger agrees, and we could start the drawings while you're typing the next lot."

"I'm typing the next lot," Tamzin said. "What a pity we can't do seven carbons at once, because we've got exactly eight copies ordered. Though I suppose really we ought to be able to count on several last-minute orders, so perhaps two lots of six would be better."

"Come on, Tamzin, get your pages in and start away. It's Page Two, of course – top right-hand corner – and the first headline is 'Violin Solo by Noted Main Street Resident'," said Roger.

"Half a minute!" said Tamzin, wrestling with tilting papers and unfamiliar levers. "There – they aren't really straight now, but it can't be helped. I only hope I've got the carbons the right way up."

"'Dunsmere people have a surprise in store'," dictated Roger.

"You bet they have," said Rissa. "D'you remember when Onion Ed was playing his Stephanie Gavotte at the Easter Fête and everyone thought it was 'God Save the Queen' and stood up?"

"Sh," said Roger. "Ready, Tamzin? What are those two Z's for?"

"Oh, help," said Tamzin. "Shall I cross them out or start again? I don't really want to juggle all those sheets of paper again."

"Back-space twice and do two X's across them," said Meryon.

"Now," said Roger, "where were we? 'Surprise in store . . . coma, because Mr Pemble, better known as Onion Ed, is already practising his famous Stephanie Gavotte for the Dunsmere Midsummer Flower Show. His violin, wrapped up in newspaper since last Easter——'"

"It was Father's *Church Times*," said Tamzin, bashing with tremendous concentration at the keys.

"Don't put that in," said Rissa.

"I'm not – idiot," said Tamzin.

"'——last Easter'," said Roger, "'has already been dusted and retuned. Our Special Correspondent was actually shown a yellowed photograph – kept in Ed's tea-caddy with the tea – of Ed himself when younger and playing with the Eckney Brass Band'."

"Hey!" said Meryon, "that word's Hackney, surely?"

"Well, he *said* Eckney," Rissa pointed out.

"It isn't what he said, it's what he meant that matters. Can you go back a few spaces, Tamzin, and type the H and A over it?"

"All right – bother – oh blast, now I've hit the asterisk thing instead: it's just above the back-spacer."

"Never mind," said Roger, "they'll think it's meant for

decoration."

"The trouble with your typing, my girl," said Rissa grinning, "is too much not letting your right hand know what your left hand doeth."

"Well, you try!" said Tamzin indignantly. "Or else get on with your pin-drawings and leave me in peace. Now, Roger?"

"'Under the photograph was written'," dictated Roger, "'How shall these dry bones live?'"

"Ought we to explain that it comes from the Bible and was meant to refer to the Brass Band instruments?" Tamzin asked doubtfully, but Meryon thought most grown-up people would grasp the idea by themselves.

"Next," said Roger, rustling his sermon-paper, "another headline: 'Fire in Well-Known Shrimper's Pants'."

"I hope it doesn't sound too disrespectful," said Tamzin. "Should we just put 'underwear'?"

"Of course not. We've got to be precise, and we've said ourselves that our news is as true as we can make it. It *was* his pants."

"All right. Go on."

"'When Mrs Shirty Smeed was airing her washing last Thursday'," said Roger, reading slowly and clearly, "'she never knew that the next time she set eyes on her son Bob's pants they would be soaring in flames'."

"It must have been awful," said Tamzin, clacking at the keys. "But she's a sensible woman. Not like Mrs Lillycrop."

"'The pants had been left with other garments'," went on Roger, "'drying on the horizontal stove-pipe in their kitchen, but while Mrs Smeed was out shopping at Mr Goldeye's the pipe grew very hot. She thinks she must have left the damper open and the fire blew up in the draught.

Unfortunately the pants were nearest to the stove and on a piece of pipe that soon was red-hot. When Mrs Smeed returned she found them wafting round the kitchen in the draught from the window, glowing and dropping burning fragments. With great presence of mind Mrs Smeed grabbed a handy shrimping-net, caught the pants and dropped them into the rainwater butt, thus averting a very nasty catastrophe'."

"Is she buying a copy?" Tamzin asked. "She ought to, with all this. And how d'you spell catastrophe?"

"She said she'd have to ask Shirty and Bob. I daresay it'll be all right. Look, here's the word: you can copy it direct."

"And then we come to 'The two Fighting Fishermen'," said Roger, "that's the headline. Now a full-stop and a new paragraph."

"Oh, *blast*!" said Tamzin, "I've hit the asterisk again."

"Let it be," said Meryon, "we can't keep having crossed-out asterisks all over the place. Put another one at the bottom of the page and think up a footnote."

Roger cleared his throat and went on, "'Westling's usual peace was somewhat shattered on Friday evening by a difference of opinion between Mr W Goddard, skipper of the *Samphire,* and Mr H Galley, skipper of the *Sarah Godden.* It seems that Mr Goddard had tied a mooring-rope in an unaccustomed place, thus causing Mr Galley to trip over it and fall flat on his face in the river mud (ten inches deep), and afterwards to hold that Mr Goddard——'"

"Why on earth can't we just say Wally," Tamzin exclaimed, "the way we usually do?"

"Because it's The Press," said Roger: "sh! – 'that Mr Goddard had done it on purpose'."

"Which I bet he did, too," said Rissa cheerfully.

"'Neither party was seriously injured'," went on Roger, "'we are thankful to say, though blows were come to'."

Meryon looked over his shoulder. "Now the footnote. Put another asterisk, Tamzin – you'll love doing that on purpose – and say, 'A return match is confidently expected'."

It was past eight o'clock when all the news items were done in duplicate on all the carbons and they got round to Mrs Grey's recipe, Meryon's story, Tamzin's verse and the editor's competition. Mrs Grey, who had been bathing Dickon (still minus the Colorado beetle) and reading to him in bed, came in to dictate her luscious and simple recipe:

APPLE FRUIT SALAD

"'Coarsely grate four sharp cooking apples into a bowl. Add the finely grated rind and the juice of one orange and sugar to taste. Make nicely juicy with extra water or squash or fruit juice. Leave for one hour or more and serve with custard or cream.' And now I'll make us all some cocoa," she said, reaching for cups from the enormous wooden dresser, "while you finish doing that page, and by the time we've had that I think you Dunsford and Winklesea people should be thinking of home."

The Shortest Ghost Story in the World was: "Two men were sitting in a railway carriage and one said to the other, 'I don't believe in ghosts, do you?' 'Oh, don't you?' said the other, and disappeared."

Under this came Tamzin's verse:

FORGOTTEN

Just an idle fishing boat forgotten by the world,
Lying lonely and deserted, sails long since furled.
Did that weed-grown, cracking hull ever swiftly glide
O'er a windswept, rolling sea, 'gainst a racing tide?
Now the old ship sits and dreams of the days long past.
Sadly I gaze on the furled-up sails and the broken mast.

"It's rather nice," said Meryon. "I didn't know you wrote things as good as that."

"It doesn't scan," said Tamzin critically, "but it'll have to do. Now we've only got the competition. Ready, Rodge?"

"'The Editor and Staff'," read Roger, "'will present a prize of a Box of Three Men's Handkerchiefs for the best and neatest written account of 'Why I like Living in Westling.' Please enter and support your local newspaper, the only paper giving only Westling news. Closing date, next Saturday. No more than one entry accepted from each Competitor'."

"Phew!" said Tamzin. "Is that really the lot? It wouldn't be so bad if we hadn't had to do it all twice over."

"I expect that's nothing to what we've got coming, now we've started this thing," said Meryon cheerfully. "What about when our circulation doubles? Or trebles? Or even quadruples?"

"There must be an easier way," said Tamzin, flexing her stiff fingers.

"If we think of one, we'll try it," said the editor. "But meanwhile we'll just have to go on as we are." He was thumbing through the neatly stacked copies, each bearing the name of the person who had ordered it. "All we've got to do now is finish the drawings and sew the pages together. I say, I wish we could deliver them tomorrow."

"I've had a thought about delivery," Tamzin said. "If we

gave him a free copy wouldn't Fred Downing at the post office deliver them with the Monday papers? I could leave them there on my way to school. If I see him at church tomorrow, I'll ask. And as to the afternoon, we're going bird-watching. At least I am, anyway. Oh, and don't forget to try for orders from your parents, because every little helps."

CHAPTER 8

Journey Over Blossoming Stones

On Sunday morning, which was heavy with white mist, Tamzin tried to keep her mind on the service and the singing and her father's excellent sermon, but it kept wandering to inconsequent things like Bob Smeed's pants, and the cost of typewriting paper, and astonishing rare birds . . . What could the castle one be? An escaped cockatoo? (It did seem, now she remembered, to have had a sort of crest.) A fabulous jungle honey bird that had lost its way? Or perhaps a bee-eater such as was so dramatically illustrated in her father's bird book and had, so said the text, only twice brought off a brood of young ones in Britain. But no, the bee-eater was a flaming coloured bird, all reds and golds and greens and blues, and their bird had been a strange un-English pink, with that noticeable barring somewhere on the wings, or back, or both, she couldn't be sure. . . .

"And now to God the Father, God the Son . . ." she suddenly heard her father say; Miss Deeprose glided back on to the organ bench and a bronchial wheeze came from the vestry where Johnny Beatup started pumping.

"Oh, help," thought Tamzin guiltily, "I don't believe I took in a word. And being up here in the choir everyone

68

could see I was dreaming." She did her very best with the last hymn, to make up, but as soon as they were all out in the windy churchyard again, under the windy, leaning pine trees, her mind was back on the news and their paper, and she was hurrying along the grass at the edge of the shingle path, past more decorous worshippers, to catch up Fred Downing whose little post-office-cum-general-store was life's worst threat to Smiling Morn.

Fred Downing was one of Westling's most respected and honourable men. He was not married, though he had been "walking out" for seven years, and he rarely did anything in the evenings more reckless than making wool rugs, he at one end and his betrothed at the other until such time as the work met in the middle.

Fred took a broadminded view of the *Westling News* and expressed himself perfectly willing to deliver it with the morning papers, "always providing that there's nothing unsuitable or libellous in it; I wouldn't want to be mixed up in anything like that, in my position of course."

Having reassured him on this point, ("Well, we showed the first edition to Dad and he said it was 'deserving of a longer life than he was afraid it would get'"), Tamzin promised to leave the first batch early in the morning: "And one is a free copy for you, Fred, for delivering them for us."

Thanking her with extreme courtesy, Fred said that what he had he always paid for, and if he cared for the paper sufficiently he would place an order in due course. Then Tamzin suddenly had what was to be one of the brainwaves of the paper's career.

"Hey, Fred! I've just thought. You wouldn't like to *advertise* in it, would you? We wouldn't charge much – I'd have to discuss that with the others – I'm sure you'd find it

69

would pay. You could put in all kinds of things, such as, 'Rice is cheap and good this week, and have you tried our genuine Indian curry powder to go with it?' After all, it must pay the big shops to advertise in the ordinary papers, mustn't it, or they wouldn't do it?"

Fred said that he would consider the matter, as he never took any step without proper consideration, and he might talk it over with Enid in the evening, over the rug. Full of high spirits and hopefulness, Tamzin bounded along down the Main Street and over the vicarage back garden wall. There would be just time to get out of her Sunday dress and into jeans and a sweater before lunch.

Mrs Grey didn't much care for Tamzin to race off immediately afterwards and catch and groom Cascade. "It isn't fair to anyone's digestion. Give it fifteen minutes, anyway."

Tamzin threw herself down on the edge of the lawn in the sunshine. First she stared up at the sky through a lacing of ash-leaves, and then she rolled over and stared at a bright green grasshopper rubbing out his strange music from his knees. Two butterfly shadows swept over the grass almost under her eyes, but when she glanced up to see the shadows' owners all she saw was Dickon gravely walking down the path with a bunch of wilted potato leaves clutched in his hands.

"Dickon," said his father, from under the scullery window where he was unstopping the drain for Mrs Grey, "that isn't *another* lot from my potato patch, I hope?"

"'Course not," said Dickon with wounded dignity. "I said I wouldn't. These are my first ones, that I keep bringing back for a drink of water. That's why they're looking so wore out."

"I was talking to Charlie Deeprose about your beetle – in

strictest confidence, of course – after church this morning,"
said the vicar, straightening the piece of wire that he was
poking down the drain. "He said it's been the law for some
years now that anyone finding a Colorado beetle must
report it to the Ministry of Agriculture."

"Even when they've lost it again?" Tamzin called, rolling
over and sitting sideways with her hands spread out on the
warm short grass.

"Yes, I'm afraid so. What has to be reported is 'any
suspected outbreak', so that Ministry experts can come
down and make a proper examination. Charlie says that if
Colorados once get a hold, and lay eggs and hatch grubs,
they can ruin a whole large field of potatoes."

"Are you going to tell about Jerusalem?" Dickon asked
uneasily, twirling his bunch of drooping leaves.

"I'm afraid I'll have to, Dicky."

"You won't tell them he's at the ferry hut, though, will
you Daddy?"

"Well . . ." The vicar wrestled with his conscience.
"Perhaps I won't unless they ask. But if they should say,
'You don't suppose he's hiding by the ferry hut, do you?' I
might have to."

"If it's being mentioned anyhow," said Tamzin, "I
suppose we could report it in the paper: 'Potato Peril No
Longer Threatens Westling', or something like that."

"It was me finding him that unthreatened it," said
Dickon, a little comforted by this great thought.

"Did you ask about the reward?" Tamzin called to her
father. She humped up her back like a camel and rose to
her feet.

"Yes. He says there used to be a reward, as Meryon
thought, but that was a long time ago. They stopped it after
people began smuggling beetles in from France, and things

like that."

"Wow! I bet old Jim would've had a go, if he'd known!" said Tamzin. "Perhaps he did."

"Charlie says some local councils still do offer small rewards at times," went on the vicar, fishing out a clump of dishmop strands from the secret places of the drain, "but he hasn't heard of one in this district lately, so perhaps we'll have to forget about a reward."

"I'd rather have Jerusalem than a reward," said Dickon, and went stumping purposefully on to the gate.

Tamzin paused on her way into the house to get a crust for catching Cascade, and peered distastefully into the gaping horrors of the drain. She was just going to say, "Dad, what is a bird that's pink and barred and has a crest and is nearly as big as a cuckoo?" when she suddenly changed her mind. It wasn't really fair to tell her parents about a thing which would lower the value of the paper to them when they bought it – like telling someone the plot of a book they were just going to read. So she rushed on through the kitchen to the sunshiny sitting-room to see if she could look it up for herself. After about five minutes of leafing the illustrations in her father's bird book, sitting in the sunshine in the window that looked down the river to the sea, Tamzin stopped at page 268. There, facing that page, was a double illustration. On one side was a pair of English Cuckoos, and on the other was a bird with cinnamon-pinkish breast and head and neck, broadly barred black and white tail and wings, and black-tipped crest. It had a long, delicate curved bill, like a curlew's and looked strange and exotic, as if it were a bird from some far-distant land. Even its name, hoopoe, was outlandish enough. . . .

"And you, live crested cockatoos,
Grave toucans, hornbills and hoopoes . . ."

"Wow!" she said to herself, overcome with awe and a wild surmise. "Oh, *wow!*"

"What did you say, dear?" called her mother from the hall, where she was putting a pile of letters on the dresser for the post.

"Oh, I was only talking to myself. . . . May I go, now, Mamariti? It must be more than fifteen minutes."

"All right, my pet. And if you see Mrs Merrow at Castle Farm, give her my love and ask how her leg is getting on, will you?"

"Yes, Mother darling! Don't wait tea if I'm late."

Cascade in his full summer coat, was as sleek and white as a plum-petal. When he saw Tamzin coming through the paddock he raised his head from the summer grass and heaved a long, snorting sigh. Unlike Rissa's Siani he never gave trouble over catching, but sometimes he expressed a human resignation to his fate, as if to say, "What, again? I only went out yesterday, and today is Sunday, when a fellow might expect a little peace."

Tamzin patted him and gave him his crust, and then a bit for little Banner who pushed with his ears back and ought not to have been humoured, but Tamzin liked all things to be equal, as far as she could make them.

Cascade got rather an absent-minded grooming because Tamzin's mind was on so many other things, but there was not much mud in the paddock, this warm dry June, and he looked perfectly well turned out as she rode him trotting up the village street.

Rissa and the boys had arranged to meet her at Castle Farm, where Cascade could be put in the Orchard with

Siani and the bird-watching carefully organised on foot. Settling into his lovely long-strided canter after they had left the village and the Beach Works behind, Cascade was soon coming up to the castle and its pools of meadow buttercups, white campion and lady's bedstraw. Tamzin swung him out seawards, so as not to pass too closely to the silent fortress and frighten away their wonderful, strange bird. She saw no sign of it as she rode by, but a kingfisher, suddenly startled, flew darting down a tide-creek as Cascade loomed whitely over the brink. It was like a jewel in all its splendid swift colours; all the Marsh, in fact, was like a jewel in this Sunday's brightness.

It was a long time since Tamzin had ridden out here, where the beach stretched yellow fingers into the grazings, and she was astonished at the summer beauty of a place normally so bare and barren. It was as if the pebbles had burst into bloom. No earth was here – not for many feet down – but everywhere Tamzin looked the beach was crowded with sea-pinks, yellow stonecrop and tiny golden broom. And all among the creeping colours, like flower arrangements on a coloured carpet, were big bold sprays of dark-blue viper's bugloss and the dragon's blood red of valerian and, once, the most lovely outburst of tiny foxgloves, high on a beach bank, so that Tamzin saw them against the blue of the sky. And such a sky! Surely no sky, unless it hung across an ocean, was ever so vast and high and wide and full of light as a Marsh sky. Here, you could see the horizon all around you, like a circle of sea-green and Marsh-green. When the sky was greeny-blue, as now, there was a strange kind of unity between earth and sea and air that surely could never be seen in any other place.

Tamzin looked at it all with the kind of warm, protective affection she always felt for it, as if the Marsh had been her personal back garden, but as soon as Cascade's ears were pointing to the farm again she had forgotten the miracle of the blossoming stones and was thinking of the wonder in the castle.

CHAPTER 9

The Fabulous Bird

In the kitchen of Castle Farm Mrs Merrow was making Fat Rascals for Sunday tea. With sleeves pushed up on strong arms, brown with gardening, she kneaded the rich, curranty dough at her big table.

"Hallo, Mrs Merrow! May we leave Cascade with Siani for a bit, please? We're walking to the castle."

"Now, Tamzin, you know you don't have to ask, surelye," said Mrs Merrow reprovingly. Then, suddenly crinkling into smiles, "Come you in when you've been to the orchard – me first batch of Rascals is due out dreckly minute, and that's when they're nicest."

"We haven't really got time," began Roger conscientiously, as editor of a very busy paper, but Mrs Merrow's Fat Rascals were something quite magical – she always used real butter – and then, as editor of a very newly founded paper, it suddenly struck him that they could use the time of eating Rascals for trying to get a Castle Farm order and some Castle Farm news. "At least, we oughtn't to have time," he added, "but as far as I'm concerned we certainly will have!"

"The way you talk!" said Mrs Merrow, getting going with her wooden rolling-pin, "anyone'd think you was working folks, and not youngsters having a nice long weekend."

"Well——" began Roger indignantly. Then, "Tell you when we come back from the orchard."

When they came back, Mrs Merrow was tidying up the long, scrubbed table. At one end of it was a wire cake-rack piled with steaming flaky circles all flushed with gold and brown like sunburned faces, and in the middle was her yellow jug of bugloss, blue as gentians.

"Where's everybody?" Tamzin asked, sprawling on a windsor chair with her elbows on the table.

Mrs Merrow rubbed her hands down her flowery apron and reached for the cake-rack. "Dad and Mike and our Joseph's all turning hay in the ten-acre. Dad he don't reckon to work much on the Sabbath, but with hay you just about have to, times. Help yourselves, loves, while I fetch a jug of milk." Between mouthfuls of hot, buttery Rascals, the editor and his staff told Mrs Merrow all about the *Westling News*. She proved an easy catch as a subscriber because, being so isolated out on the Marsh, the best bits of local news quite often passed her by and she dearly loved a gossip, with perhaps a little scandal thrown in for flavour. But, for the same reason, she was not much use as a source of information.

"Anything happened, you say? Well now, things is always happening, loves, but at my time of life I just do incline to disremember. Did I tell you what our dad said when I forgot what day of the week it was? He said, 'Mam, you've surelye got a powerful forgettery'! Now Roger, you can reach the Rascals; don't wait to be asked, lad. You're another one like Joseph, I know, what can eat forever of cake and never feel the difference. Oh – but tell you one bit of news for your paper! You know my old black hen, that's nine year old if she's a day? Well, she laid an egg last Tuesday as weighed ten ounces on these very kitchen scales, I tell you true, and inside was four good yolks and another whole egg with a shell on! That made a good scrambled egg breakfast for all four of us. But the ole girl she hasn't laid since. Nor she didn't lay for a month before. Not that you can really wonder, can you?"

Meryon had extracted his notebook from his trousers pocket and was jotting all this down while Roger finished his third Rascal and second mug of milk.

"Perhaps we could put it in Nature Notes," suggested Tamzin.

"Are hens Nature?" Meryon asked.

Rissa said she thought they were all too natural, judging by the ones their neighbours kept just over their fence, which were natural at half-past four in the morning, but Tamzin lost interest in the argument and began to agitate for starting out to the castle. No one said what they were going there for, and Mrs Merrow didn't ask but sent her love to Mrs Grey in return for hers, and asked to have her paper left with Smiling Morn who delivered the farm groceries every Thursday.

On the walk to the castle everyone spoke with hushed voices, as though the fabulous bird they hoped to see there might be able to hear them across a quarter mile of grazings. Tamzin's account of the hoopoe in her father's bird book was carefully listened to.

"It does sound very like it," Roger said. "What did the book say about them? Are they really very rare?"

"I didn't stop to read it. I wanted to hurry and get out here. But I can look it up again this evening."

"The main thing is having a really good view of it this afternoon," said Meryon. "You two frightened it yesterday, blundering into the castle on horseback the way you did. We've got to organise things better, today."

"Two of us in and two out," suggested Rissa.

"It flew out over the seaward wall," said Roger.

"From the middle keep," said Tamzin, "but we didn't see exactly where."

"Supposing we have all you three outside, spaced under the seaward wall," said Meryon, "because it's when the bird is outside the castle that it'll be most difficult to follow. Then I'll go inside, very quietly, and see what I can see. If it is disturbed, even with one quiet person creeping round, it'll almost certainly fly outside, and then there'll be three of you to look at it carefully and see exactly where it goes."

"Well, I suppose so," said Rissa a little grudgingly, because it would seem more fun to be inside than simply waiting under the wall.

"Meryon's easily the best climber," Tamzin said, "and whoever goes inside may have to climb the middle keep – I mean, if the bird just doesn't appear at all. But don't frighten it, will you, Meryon? I'd rather we didn't find out anything about it at all than frighten it away if it's thinking of making a nest."

"Hoopoes don't nest in Britain," Rissa said positively. "They only sometimes – very rarely – fly over. Like golden orioles. Once in a while you see a letter in the paper saying that someone's seen one in their garden, but never anything more than that."

"Well, whatever it's doing, I won't frighten it if I can possibly help it," sid Meryon. "What I really want is for it not to know I'm there. And we don't want it to know you lot are there, either, so no loud songs, mouth organ obligatoes or yelling!"

Rissa gave him a crushing look but no one else took any

notice and, as they were nearing the castle now, there was no more talk except in whispers. Meryon left them at the gateway and went silently through the broken gap while the other three settled themselves in well-spaced places under the seaward wall. Far from being able to whisper to each other they could not even see each other, because of the great bastions that swung out from the walls all round: there were five of them, like the five points of a star, but rounded. Tamzin settled herself in a wind-sheltered corner where a bastion met the intersecting curtain-wall and prepared to enjoy the warmth of the sun, and the sounds of larks and seagulls, and the dazzle of shorn sheep and lambs against jewelled grass. But almost at once she saw the hoopoe. That it was in fact a hoopoe there was no doubt at all. There, swooping slowly towards a flowering hawthorn close to Tamzin's bastion was the same fabulous bird whose pictures she had seen in the bird book.

Tamzin's heart gave a great jump of excitement. She wanted to shout out in case the others hadn't seen the wonder, but scarcely dared to breathe. And then, as if to show her every detail of its rareness and its beauty, the hoopoe settled on a branch of the thorn tree. A small scatter of white petals, dislodged by its landing, floated lightly away on the wind: the bird raised and lowered its crest, that looked so like a Red Indian's black-tipped headdress, and swooped up to and over the wall. Tamzin let out a sudden long breath and felt her heart going faster. She wondered what the bird had been carrying in that delicate curved bill. Some small thing was in it, she was sure. Perhaps a caterpillar or a worm? Then, if so, perhaps the bird was nesting? That really would be historic! A news item to beat all news items for years to come.

Her speculations didn't last long because, with a sudden

gliding dive, the hoopoe came over the wall again just to the left of where she was crouching and went away on the wind towards a clump of swaying willows, by one of the innumerable wide ditches that criss-crossed the whole of the Marsh, serving doubly for drains and fences. Then, marvel of marvels, from the small jungle of leaning willow trees it called its own name: "Hoopoo-ooe, hoopoo-ooe!"

Tamzin began to crawl round the bastion in search of Rissa or Roger, excitement bumping round inside her chest. But she had scarcely covered three yards when the bird was racing back again with its strange undulating flight, and Tamzin stopped and "froze" against the stones. You could hardly believe that it was the same bird, she said to herself, astonished by all this incredible good fortune – and with another worm or grub, she noticed, as it soared above the wall. Perhaps there were *two* birds? A nesting pair? What a scoop that would be. But just as she was thinking this, Tamzin's solitary exultation was crudely shattered, and again she could scarcely believe her own goggling eyes, for there across the short grass in front of her went running and stumbling and panting, and looking back nervously, a middle-aged female artist with her stool and easel and painting gear under her arms. Quite obviously she had come from the castle. But why? And what was she so plainly afraid of? Not the hoopoes? Surely, oh surely not Meryon? Tamzin had half-risen, with the idea of going to find out, when the quiet Marsh air was suddenly torn with anxious shouts, and she saw to her horror and despair that the artist female had run herself to a stop between the castle and the willows and was calling at the top of her voice, "George! George!" and waving a flaming scarlet headscarf like a signal of distress towards the shore.

"Oh, hell's bells!" said Roger, coming round the bastion,

"that's torn it."

"You saw them? The hoopoes?" Tamzin asked.

"Of course I did. So did Rissa. She's gone round the other way to see what frightened the old girl."

"But Roger, we can't let her go on making all that uproar near the hoopoes!"

"We can't very well stop her, until we know what frightened her – or until George comes to rescue her. Come on quickly!"

They ran round the castle to the gateway, shocking still further a group of sheep who had just got over the shock of the fleeing artist. Meryon was standing at the low, dark entrance to one of Cloudesley Castle's caved-in vaults, brushing himself down and talking to Rissa.

"I simply couldn't think of any other way to get her out," he was saying. "How was I to know that she was going to go berserk and run screaming? All I did was to creep into the vault without her seeing me – she was sitting there, painting that wall, I don't know why: it only looks like a wall to me. I crawled along inside the vault until I thought I was as near as I could get to her, and then I began scraping one stone on another, and sometimes tapping them, you know. The idea was to make her feel a bit uneasy, being all alone there, and what I thought was that she'd probably just go away and do her painting somewhere else."

"She went away, all right!" said Rissa. "I never saw an artist run so fast."

"You could have *asked* her to go, first," suggested Tamzin.

"And do you think she would have? What reason could I have given? If I'd mentioned the birds, she'd have wanted to see them just as much as we do."

"Well, listen to her now!" said Tamzin. "D'you know

where she is? Just between the castle and the hoopoe's trees."

Meryon stared at her. "The hoopoe's trees? D'you mean to say you've seen it?"

"All three of us," said Roger. "Several times."

"I think there were two: a nesting pair," said Tamzin. "Oh, help! Can't we do anything about that awful woman?"

"If we do," said Rissa, "she'll know we were around the castle and connect us with the knocking in the vaults. She might easily sue Meryon. I expect you can, for being given a really bad fright."

"I didn't mean to frighten her," said Meryon, "only I didn't realise she was so easily upset. But I really wish I'd seen the hoopoes, too. Of course, I was grovelling in the bowels of the earth when you people were gazing at the wonder."

"They won't come back while she's hollering for her George," said Rissa, disgusted.

"But *is* she? She isn't hollering now, anyway."

With a single idea they all made a dash at the steep grassy mound where it swept up to the top of the seaward wall, and near the top they dropped down and started crawling, so that presently four heads only might have been seen among the wallflowers that flaunted there, if anyone had been looking very closely. But no one was.

"Good gracious!" said Rissa, "he's taken her in his arms. I thought she looked too old for all that, didn't you?"

"I expect it's worse, if they get it when they're older, like measles," said Meryon sagely. "Anyway, there's a proverb that says 'There's no fool like an old fool'".

"It isn't that I mind them being in love," said Rissa, "it's their being in love just *there*."

"They're bound to move off presently," said Roger tolerantly. "I expect she's had to tell him all about the terror in the castle, and now he's telling her all about his nice walk on the shore, and then he'll pick up her things for her and they'll walk off for a cosy tea in a Winklesea Olde Tea Shoppe."

"He's picking up her things, all right," said Tamzin, "but just look!"

"Oh, no!" said Rissa. "My sainted aunt, not a picnic, and just there!"

"Oh well," said Meryon philosophically, "it looks to me as if that is about that, and the hoopoes will close down till after tea. We may as well go back to the farm. Probably Mr Merrow and Mike and Joseph would be glad for some help in the hayfield."

"It doesn't really matter, I suppose," said Tamzin, "now we have positively seen them. The only thing we don't know for certain is whether they're nesting here, but we do know they're here. And we can always come out again in the evenings, before the next issue goes to print."

"It'd be the sort of news that *any* paper would be glad to have," Rissa said, as they began to slither backwards down the top part of the slope. "Hardly anybody in Britain can ever have seen a hoopoe, I should think."

"I wonder if we're really doing the right thing, though, to put it in the paper." Meryon looked a little uneasy as they walked through the castle to the gateway.

"I mean, from the hoopoes' point of view. Oh, I expect it'll be all right, but I just wondered if anyone might want to hurt them."

"Oh, surely not!" said Tamzin. "Why should anyone want to? They aren't pests, with a price on their lives, like poor Dicky's Colorado. Some people might walk out to look at them, I suppose, but they don't seem to mind that. They flew nearly over my head without bothering in the least."

"And people seeing them will only prove the genuineness of our news," said Roger. "Otherwise it *could* look as if we made up rarities just for news value. After all, no one's very likely to find a Colorado now. They'll only have our word for that."

"I think Jerusalem was just a stray one," Tamzin said, "and Dicky caught him before he had time to lay eggs or anything – I mean, if he was a she, of course."

"Perhaps it wasn't really such a coincidence as it seems," said Meryon, swinging after them through the castle gateway, "the Colorado and the hoopoes coming over in the same week. Perhaps the kind of weather conditions that carried a beetle across the channel might encourage a bird to drift northwards, too."

"I tell you one thing," said Roger after a minute or two, when they were striding down the sheep-track to the farm. "An hour or so's haymaking leads straight to one of Mrs Merrow's epic teas."

CHAPTER 10

Crisis With a Wheelchair

The haymaking was a pure delight of heady, hot clover smells and cheerful shouting, all under a high metallic sun, and Mrs Merrow's tea was well up to standard, including as it did a bowl of thick yellow cream and farm strawberry jam. It was nice seeing Mike again, the tough, dark elder son who was as much a part of the earth and farming as Jim Decks was of the sea; and it was even nicer seeing young Joseph, whom Mrs Merrow had lovingly adopted from the world's old rubbish heap with all his roughness and his swearing and his dirt. He was believed to be "about thirteen" and, after a period of moodiness and suspicion, was just beginning to settle happily at the farm and to accept the fact (incredible though it may have seemed to him) that the Merrows really loved him for himself and not for what they might get out of him.

When everyone had helped to clear the table after tea and wash up, Tamzin turned from rinsing down the sink and said with a contented sigh, "What a good thing I thought of telling Mother not to wait tea. She'll know we're here, so we really needn't hurry back. Unless you have to, Rissa?"

"No one ever expects me back when I'm with you," said

Rissa.

Tamzin was drying her hands on the towel that hung on the open back door. "And Roger's and Meryon's parents never mind anyway, so what about all going back to the castle for another investigation? Joseph too, of course. You'd like to come, wouldn't you, Joseph?"

"Investigating what?" asked Joseph cautiously. He had reason to know more than most people did about Tamzin's tendency to wild ideas.

"We'll tell you on the way, because it's a secret. I don't mean a *real* secret from you and Mr Merrow," she hastily explained to the farmer's wife, "but a secret until you read about it in the paper."

"It doesn't matter about Joseph," said Meryon, grinning at him. "He can be a reporter, the same as us, slaving for Roger."

"I perishing well slave, too, editor or not," protested Roger.

"Well, I got to feed the pigs first . . ." Joseph was still shy and inclined to be solitary.

"We'll help," Rissa said, "and get the cows in for Mike, too."

"Hey, what about rounding up the ewes and lambs for me?" demanded Mr Merrow, who was sitting on the bench outside in the westering sunshine with his dogs, smoking his pipe and listening to the conversation as it floated through the door.

"Why ever not?" asked Tamzin. "We've got Cascade and Siani, though we can't very well use Patsy and Star after they've been working so hard pulling hay. And it doesn't take five to feed six pigs."

"Garn, gal! I can round up me own sheep, surely. Howsumever, you can help me if you like. I must say me ole knees is stiff arter all that haying."

Five minutes later the farmhouse kitchen was empty, except for Mrs Merrow sitting comfortably at the table with her glasses on and her mending before her, three cats sprawled in summer abandon on the coloured rag rug, and the great black kettle on the vast black stove, its curved spout hissing perpetually like a willing and domesticated serpent.

One way and another it was rather late when they all arrived at the castle, and though they were as quiet and soft-moving as five people can be, they never saw the hoopoes.

"Perhaps it's just too late," Tamzin suggested, still whispering though they were now some yards from the castle and walking back to the farm. "Perhaps they've gone to bed."

"Hens go terribly early, if that's anything to go by," said Rissa. "I expect that's why the silly things rouse up so early, too."

"I dunno," said Joseph, his funny squashed nose wrinkling up with thought. "Sounds an odd sort of bird to me. A feller in a boat I were in once had a cockatoo in a cage. You shouldn't think it were something of that kind, should you, what escaped?"

"No," said Tamzin. "It was a hoopoe – a pair of hoopoes, I think. They must be somewhere about. They wouldn't leave for a very small picnic, especially if they've got a nest. Look, we'll try to get out here in the evenings, before next weekend, and see what we've got to report on Saturday morning."

"As well as hunting for other news?" Meryon asked. "There won't be much time. But I might manage once or twice. Homework is getting pretty heavy now, for the exams."

"And we've still got the wether tegs to shear, after the last of the hay is in," said Joseph. "But I'll nip down when I can. Lord! I never thought to see meself a birdwatcher, nor I did!"

"That's one of the nicest things about life," said Tamzin, "never knowing what you'll find yourself doing next."

Curiously enough, almost the very next thing she was doing, broadly speaking, was rescuing old Jim Decks from his first crisis with the motorised wheelchair. Tamzin had been cheerfully cantering homewards over the levels, the low sun sending her and Cascade's shadows out in front of them like a very long-eared horse and a rider as tall as a tree. Perhaps she did hear the engine of Jim's chair, but if she did she took no notice of it. There were other vehicles in Westling – for example, there was Onion Ed's Silver Bullet. This was a decrepit-looking motorbike with a most magnificent bullet-shaped sidecar, all painted shining aluminium, that Ed had picked up in a breaker's yard and now used to fetch his vegetables from Dunsford. The motorbike could do nearly four miles an hour down the bumpy Westling road – it had been known to do five in Dunsford – and the vicar loved to tell the tale (very discreetly, of course) of how he was once walking home to Westling with the Silver Bullet chugging steadily behind him all the way. Ed Pemble caught him up just by the village green and leaned out to shout above the roaring of his bike, "I'd have given you a lift, Vicar, if I could've caught you up."

But Jim Decks's invalid chair was obviously in a quite different class from the Silver Bullet. Her father had said that it could go quite fast on a good flat road. Well, here it was, properly ditched at the roadside and the ferryman ranting and cursing beside it while he jabbed and poked angrily at it with one of a pair of crutches he had unaccountably come by. Tamzin pulled up Cascade at the road gate and leaned down to open it. Once through, the pony was so shocked at being turned away from home that he stood still and snorted, and then turned his head right round to look at Tamzin in reproachful disbelief. But she made him go on along the grass verge to the place of disaster, and then pulled him up and looked anxiously at Jim. He seemed all right, hopping around without the use of the crutches, or even of his stick, but he was so absorbed in his fury that he never heard Cascade's hoofs on the grass.

"Jim – can I do anything?"

"Eh, gorblimey, gal, jumping out on a feller like that!"

"I didn't jump out: you just didn't hear me coming."

"As if I didden have enough trouble without being give shocks by them as ought to know better."

"Well, as long as you aren't hurt," said Tamzin practically, "we'd better see what we can do about the chair, I suppose. It's a good thing this ditch is fairly dry – in a wet summer you'd have been sailing." She jumped down and began tying Cascade's reins to the fence, knowing perfectly well that this isn't a horsemanlike thing to do, as Cascade probably did as well but he was too much of a gentleman to take advantage of it.

Having got over the shock of her arrival, old Jim started roaring and cursing again with even greater zest because of having an audience.

"The doctor said, didden 'e, if you open her up on a straight road, Jim, he said, you'll be in Dunsford afore you've properly left Westling, he said. An' whur am I, gal? I ask you that, and now I tellee – in the blessed ditch-'ole, same as a ruddy tadpole, and me tarnation goo-chair on top of me."

"Well, not really on top of you, Jim," said Tamzin, reasonably enough since he was hopping about all round it. "Now, let's both give it a shove together."

"I tellee, her'd a-bin on top if I give her half a chance," said Jim. "She'd only to 'ave done a liddle lurch and she'd a-done it. But I didden let her, see, the ole baggage. And I tellee another thing, you carsn't shift her. She's a tedious great weight for all she looks so flighty, gal."

Jim was right about this, because their combined efforts produced no more than a strange and inexplicable sigh, somewhere deep within the works.

Tamzin straightened herself and pushed her hair back over her shoulders. "I suppose you haven't got a length of rope, Jim?" she suddenly asked, hardly daring to hope that he could have such a thing, in this unlikely place.

The ferryman glared at her. "'Course I gotta length of rope. You don't sposen as I – seafaring man – ud go voyaging without the needful, do you?" He was grovelling under the seat of the vehicle, now. "I gotta anchor, what's more. That were half me trouble. 'Er didden hold on the hard road, see, and when 'er did hold, 'er held too sudden. I lay I'll git the ole *Emma* back and have her done up proper, so I will. Rope," he announced, finding it and hauling it out.

"What on earth d'you want to throw out an anchor for, when you've got perfectly good brakes? Really, Jim!" She took the rope. "What a stroke of luck. And such a good long piece. D'you think we could pull it out with Cascade?"

The old man considered the pony in a pessimistic manner. "He ent got nuthen for you to belay the rope on, gal."

"Well, honestly, Jim, you don't expect him to have cleats and belaying-pins and bollards sticking out, do you? I think, if we run it through the stirrup-irons . . . and round his chest . . . it ought to do. I'd have to pad the rope with something, though, and I haven't got a sweater on, today, it's been so warm." She looked speculatively at old Jim's navy guernsey, that he had knitted himself in a traditional Sussex pattern.

"Ah, I know what you're thinking, ole young 'un. Gor, darn take it, even the clothes orf me back." But he was hauling it over his head, his shining earrings and dazzle of hair and beard disappearing into its folds, so that he looked, for a moment, exactly like any ordinary seaman of any middling age, instead of the flamboyant lawless old sailor that he was.

"After all," said Tamzin, posting the rope-end through Cascade's off-side iron, "it's all for your sake. It doesn't really matter to me if the invalid-chair stays in the ditch till Christmas – except that I'd be sorry for you not to be able to use it."

"And calling me a invalid," grumbled Jim, though melting a little now. He knew Tamzin well enough to know that she would really be sorry if he couldn't use his chair. "Here, gimme the other end, gal," he said, roughly gentle, "an' I'll make un fast to the blessed bows. Gor, sink me for a coghead, but I never reckoned as I'd see the day I'd be shipwrecked in Char Deeprose's ole road-dik, that I never. An' I tellee, I bin wrecked in a dunnamany odd places, time I went foreign. There was a time, once, when I come-to on a great ole seashore and found meself being wep' over by one of them fantastical giraffe-women – you know, with hundreds of gold collars round throats a yard high. Fell in love at first sight, she did – I wunt bad-looking

92

in them days, you unnerstand – and the Chief's favourite daughter, too, and black as a bilge. Cor, but I thought I'd never git away and see me home and folks no more. But I tellee how I did it——"

"Yes, Jim, I'd awfully like to hear, but it's getting late now, and I've still got a bit of homework to do: could you give a haul when I say 'ready', in case Cascade can't move it by himself? It's really deeply bogged in."

Between them all they managed first to rock the astonishingly heavy invalid carriage a little, to the accompaniment of a loud sucking kind of noise, and then suddenly to dislodge it completely and rush it out and right on to the road. There was one dreadful moment when Tamzin was also lending a hand at pushing, and so no one was at Cascade's head, and it suddenly seemed likely that he was going to tear off all the way to Dunsford with the wheelchair in tow, but Tamzin hauled herself up the rope to his head again and stopped him after only seven or eight yards.

Jim Decks tested the engine while Tamzin unfastened the tow-rope and guernesy, and it made all the proper noises and responses. But she waited until he had got the chair going, and headed safely up the road again, its scarlet L-plate glaring like a rear-light, before she rode off clattering down the Main Street to home and supper.

School again tomorrow, she thought, sighing a little to herself as she rubbed Cascade down in the stable-yard and led him back to the paddock and Banner. But it'll be the very first day of the very first issue of the very first Westling newspaper. And already we've got at least three more items for next week.

Going in at the back door, hungrily sniffing, she passed a jam-jar on the scullery table and saw that it was full of wilted potato leaves. That reminds me, she said to herself, making a mental note, I've got to rough out the Colorado article some time this evening. Poor Dicky! It looks as if he hasn't found Jerusalem. I suppose I'd feel the same as he does, if we lost the hoopoes.

CHAPTER 11

Dual Hunt

It was a busy week, crammed right up to the last
half-minute, or so it seemed to one, at least, of the four
who were now attempting to combine life as newspaper
proprietors with life at school and with the ordinary daily
jobs that everyone always has to fit in somehow.

Tamzin never very much minded getting up early, and
she did this now in order to do any tack-cleaning and
room-tidying and filling up the ponies' water tank, and
even, sometimes, finishing some left-over homework,
before breakfast. That left the evenings for such homework
as could not be dealt with properly in the school dinner
hour, and for her own essential mending (she was expected
at least to sew on her own buttons) and then for a whirl of
reporting and writing-up for the *Westling News*. With all
this, and the fact that the weather broke and it poured with
rain on Tuesday and Wednesday she only managed to get
out to the castle twice; once on Monday and once on
Friday.

The first time she went, cantering out over the levels on a
clouding evening, it was fairly late because she and Rissa
had called at Mr Henzie's cake shop after school and it had
taken them longer than they expected to get him to agree

to their plan. This was that he on his part should not bother old Jim with demands for payment of damages, or allow any police intervention, and that they on their part would promise to pay off the whole sum in regular weekly instalments of whatever could be raised, and a little over as interest because of his having to wait longer for the debt to be cleared. Perhaps it was a result of her consequent lateness, but on this journey to the castle Tamzin didn't see anything at all – no hoopoes, no other watchers, no strangers even – nothing but the everlasting Romney Marsh sheep, that had always been a part of the Marsh ever since it had been snatched from the sea-bed, and fairly certainly always would be.

Tamzin tied Cascade to a thorn-tree that grew near the castle gateway and spent a full hour of silent watching and investigation inside the walls, but the only birds she saw were pigeons and jackdaws, flapping and fluttering in their noisy way about the walls, and a lark that almost wasn't a bird at all but only a song in the cloudy sky. Unhitching Cascade, Tamzin rode to the flowering may tree where the hoopoe had perched and lifted its crest before soaring up over the wall, and then she rode out to the wild-haired willows, but there was no sign of any fabulous strange bird, or that any had ever been there. Disappointed, Tamzin rode home, under the first scatter of raindrops, and just found time before bed to write about:

NARROW ESCAPE BY WESTLING FERRYMAN

"Our readers will, I'm sure, be thankful to hear that Mr J Decks (Snr.) had a happy escape from injury on Sunday evening, when out on a maiden voyage in his new motor wheelchair, which left the road and came to land in Mr C Deeprose's ditch, just beyond the Beach Works. A passing horsewoman [Well, I suppose I was, said Tamzin to herself] hitched her pony to the wheelchair and pulled it out. Apart from a little natural annoyance about the incident, Mr Decks seemed not to be disturbed and resumed his drive."

After this she added: "Note: subscriptions. Will all subscribers, if any, who have not yet paid for last week's paper please do so as soon as possible, leaving their money with Mr F Downing at the post office, because we have to buy our paper for the next issue out of our profits from the last."

Then partly to encourage other advertisers and partly because you could hardly charge old Jim for advertising when the whole paper was in aid of him, she put a paragraph in for him, free, hoping that Roger would duly approve. She wrote:

"It pays to advertise in our paper: very large circulation of eight already, daily going up; charges reasonable and sample below.

"*Westling Ferry*. There is no better way of getting across the river unless you have a boat of your own or like swimming in your clothes. Patronise the Westling Ferry, the best one and the only one on the whole of the River. Have you tried it? If not, why not? Remedy this at once."

"Well, that's made a start on Number Two, anyway," she said to her mother who came into the kitchen to say did she know that it was nine o'clock.

At school the next day Tamzin and Rissa discussed in anxious undertones, whenever they could, the non-appearance of the hoopoes. Tamzin had always been inclined to take a tragic view of things in doubt, and was plunged in gloomy foreboding, but Rissa was optimistic and very practical by nature and was never influenced by Tamzin's despair.

"They'll be there on Saturday, all right, when we get there in broad daylight. Not that I see what all the fuss is about, anyhow: there's lots of other news, just as exciting – probably more exciting from the villagers' point of view. I don't suppose many of them care very much about birds, really, do you?"

On Tuesday evening Tamzin buttoned herself up again in waterproofs still damp after cycling back from school and went to see Fred Downing before his shop closed for the night. Fred was in a cheerful mood because tomorrow was early closing and he and Enid were going to Hastings. He smiled at Tamzin, who was dripping water all over his shop floor, opened a drawer in the counter and slapped down a clatter of coins in front of her.

"Everybody paid up punctual – that was Mrs Gudgeon, Mrs Clench, Ed Pemble and Mrs Beatup, and me and Enid because we thought we'd like to take it after all, since you say it's for such a good cause. And the two we had left over we sold easily over the counter – could've sold twice as many and no trouble. So I think you could print a few more, Miss, for next Monday, don't you?"

"Oh, that's terrific," said Tamzin, picking up the coins, "everyone else will be thrilled. That means we've sold the whole dozen, with Mother's and Mrs Briggs's and Mrs Merrow's and Doctor Hargreaves's copies. Though I suppose we may have to spend about half the takings on paper."

"What about your wages bill?" Fred asked, but Tamzin said they didn't have one, neither the editor nor his reporters having any salaries at all, and not expecting any. Then, getting round to the question of advertising, she found Fred very amenable and willing to pay for a weekly paragraph. They worked one out together that went like this:

"Don't let flies invite themselves to tea at your house! And don't have old-fashioned fly-papers that catch YOU as often as the flies. Try our new up-to-the-minute Fly Spray, in special spray-top tins (no other shop in Westling keeps this line)."

"Smiling Morn – I mean Mr Goldeye will hate that," said Tamzin, because his was the only other shop in Westling and, as she and Roger had noticed on the Saturday, he had at the moment a fly-paper window display.

Fred said he didn't think they need worry about that, and, anyway, next week they could change the advertisement to one about, say, Instant Summer Puddings which saved a lot of fuel and work in all the hot weather.

"If the hot weather does come back," said Tamzin wistfully, and turned to go home and tackle an essay on Longfellow's *Hiawatha*.

Calling in at Smiling Morn's, she failed utterly either to get him to place an order for the paper or to put an advertisement in its pages. The fact that Fred Downing had done both was no encouragement to him, as Tamzin had hoped it might be, but rather the reverse, since Mr Goldeye did not care to lower himself by following the example of his rival.

"Well, I'm really sorry," said Tamzin, "because I think Mrs Goldeye would have enjoyed it and your advertisement would have helped the paper but never mind . . . You won't forget to send Mrs Merrow's out with her groceries on Thursday, will you, Mr Goldeye?" And then it suddenly struck her that there it was, Mrs Merrow's copy, sitting in the shop for a whole three-and-a-half days. Time enough for both Mr and Mrs Goldeye to read it right through three times forwards and twice backwards: and there was nothing that she could do about it; not this week, anyway, though next week she could drop the copy in on Thursday morning: and then probably she would see the Goldeyes putting in an order of their own.

On Thursday evening, with the rain still falling though less interminably, Tamzin went round the village on the dual hunt for more news and more subscribers. On the whole this pilgrimage was a successful one, though there was one awful moment when a home-made doorbell came right out in her hands, down at the Coastguard Houses, and the resulting ill-feeling prevented her from getting an order from Mr Grumbitt, the Chief Coastguard. She was loudly rebuffed at the house of one Mrs Venus, who was usually known in the vicarage as Mrs One-Who-Knows, because of a habit she had of sending anonymous letters to the vicar about all the hypocrites who went to church (which was why Mrs Venus didn't), signed One Who Knows. But there was not much point in all this secrecy since Mrs Venus always stopped the vicar when she saw him and asked, "I hope you got my letter, Vicar? I thought if nobody else was going to tell you about all those snakes-in-the-grass, I'd better."

Mrs Venus was almost abusive to Tamzin (who had nothing at all to do with feuds and skirmishes) and said that the less gossip there was going round the place, the better; and then went straight indoors to write another anonymous letter to the vicar about her neighbour, Mrs Apps.

But all Tamzin's calls were not as discouraging as these. She was most kindly received by the Deeproses at Harbour Farm, as she always was there, being asked indoors and fussed by old Mrs Deeprose and offered fudge by Miss

Deeprose and gently teased by Charlie who was the choirmaster and knew her fairly well. Old Mr Deeprose, who was a very distinguished-looking man with iron-grey hair, asked her if they were competing with the Parish Magazine and, if so, what was her father going to think? But he wasn't being serious either, and was presently giving her a delightful piece of news about a Rhode Island hen they had who was mothering two kittens which had been deserted by their own mother, folding her wings over them every night and tucking them in firmly but gently with her beak.

The Deeproses placed an order at once for the *Westling News* and said that they were sorry to have missed the very first issue. Tamzin said she would try to get a used one from someone who had finished with it, for them, because she simply couldn't bring herself to offer to type out another whole copy, even for eighteen pence extra in Jim's Cake Fund.

On Friday the sun came up through a delicate haze of mist which it soon burned away, and there was the hot bright world of summer again, but steaming after the rain. Tamzin imagined, when she was cycling to school, that it was millions and millions of years ago and the earth still cooling after the glories of being a star. But soon she was thinking about the hoopoes and how she was going to ride out and look for them again after school and tea.

But there was another excitement waiting to come in between her and the hoopoes. When she got home again at Friday tea-time, with her blazer strapped over the handle-bars because of the glorious return of hot blue weather, and her spirits high because of no more school till Monday and at least two whole evenings to spread her homework in, Dickon came rushing to meet her at the bicycle shed.

"I say, Tamzin, you're in the paper."

"I know I am," said Tamzin, unstrapping her blazer, "but I could hardly help it, being mixed up in the local news. Come to that, you'll soon be in it yourself, now you've let us do a write-up about Jerusalem."

"I don't mean *that* paper," said Dickon dismissingly. "Oh, and the beetle men have been, today. They spent nearly all morning looking at our potatoes, and all afternoon looking at other people's, but they didn't find him either, and nor have I." His voice trailed a little sadly.

"Oh, I'm sorry," said Tamzin sympathetically, walking with him to the house, swinging her school bag which was weighted with a new packet of typing paper, bought with a part of their first profits that had been regretfully withheld from Mr Henzie's little share. "But don't lose hope. *Nil desperandum,* as Meryon would say." Suddenly remembering, she added, "Well, what paper did you mean?"

"Oh yes – it's in the Local Rag, and there's lots about you and the others and the *Westling News*."

"What? Really?" Tamzin was too staggered by this unexpected development to know what she thought. "Well, I expect it might be a good thing: publicity and all that, you know. It rather depends on what they said. They weren't making fun of us, were they?" This was a terrible thought, but it was a thing grown-ups were very liable to do and you had to expect it. They rarely realised, it seemed, how funny they sometimes appeared to their youngers, but lots of quite serious things their youngers did were excruciatingly comical to them. Luckily, the immediate relations of both Tamzin and her friends were fairly immune from this kind of behaviour, but with grown-ups generally you never could tell. And there was something awfully belittling about being laughed at in this way, that made you feel foolish and the thing you were doing look ridiculous, so that you lost interest in it for ever more.

"Hallo, Tamzin!" her mother called from the kitchen as they came in at the open front door, past the ship's lifebelt that had washed up from the wreck of the *Alcantara* and was now propped in the porch, and past the umbrella stand in which Dickon was keeping six snails and two very long centipedes that ran circles round the snails. "Come and look at the *Sussex Herald*. You're in the news!"

Whirling into the kitchen Tamzin threw her school bag on to a chair and grabbed her mother round the waist and gave her a big hug and a kiss. "Where's the paper? How on earth did they ever hear about ours?"

Mrs Grey picked up the *Herald* from the big, china-laden dresser and spread it out on the table under the window. "There you are; 'Rival Weekly at Westling'. I don't know how they came to hear of it."

"Read it aloud," said Dickon. "I've only heard it once."

Tamzin obliged. "'It has come to our notice that a rival weekly paper has begun production at Westling, near Dunsford; *The Westling News*. This enterprising paper is edited by a schoolboy, Roger Lambert, whose idea it was, and the four regular reporters range in age from six to sixteen.'"

"That's me, isn't it?" said Dickon glowingly, "The one that's six."

"You haven't found us much news yet – sh!" said Tamzin, then raising her voice for reading again: "'The publication offices are in the stable loft at Westling Vicarage, and we understand that the vicar doesn't reckon to get much use out of his typewriter on Saturdays. The charge for four well-packed pages is eighteen pence (all profits devoted to charity) and the news provided is strictly

Parish News Only, though we notice that news is not by any means the only fare offered. Readers may find in this first issue, a competition (with prize), an excellent and seasonal recipe (we have tried it), a poem, a very short story, and several pithy thumbnail drawings. We are relieved to read that the *Westling News* has no intention of competing with any other newspaper until such time as another paper devotes itself exclusively to Westling news as we feel that our position might become somewhat precarious were Roger Lambert and his able staff to begin directing their talents in a wider field'."

"Well, what d'you think of that?" asked Mrs Grey. "Fame at last!"

"I suppose it's all right," said Tamzin doubtfully. "Of course, it's rather fun being in the news at all, but they *are* making fun of our paper, even if only a little. I was afraid they would, when Dickon told me."

"You mustn't mind being laughed at, pet," said her mother, lifting the big brown teapot from the dresser and putting it to warm at the edge of the stove. "In fact, one of the best things to learn is how to laugh at yourself."

"It isn't so much that I mind them making fun of *me*," said Tamzin, folding the paper, "or of any of us. But the paper was meant to be serious. It doesn't matter," she added sensibly, "it could have been a lot worse. What is there for tea, Mamariti darling? I'm simply wasting away with famine. I do hope toast!"

"Not in a June heatwave, you donkey!" Mrs Grey smiled at her. "But there is a strawberry shortcake——"

"Ah!" said Tamzin, but Dickon only grinned, because he knew.

"And glasses of cold chocolate——"

"Oh!" said Tamzin, "I simply can't wait." And she

dashed into the scullery to wash her hands.

"It's in the garden," her mother called, "on the side lawn."

"Perfect! I'll carry some things out, if you'll leave whatever needs carrying on the table."

After a tea like that, under a sun like that, it would have been nice to stay sprawled on the groundsheet on her back, staring at the sky and the trees and the birds and the drifting smoke from Smiling Morn's chimney, but after a minute or two Tamzin jumped up. If the trouble with seeing the hoopoes had been because of getting there too late, she was, this evening, going to get there early.

"Tamzin dear, don't forget you've just had tea – and a fairly enormous one," said her mother, glancing up from covering the honey against assembling bees and flies.

"I won't forget!" called Tamzin, walking slowly and deliberately down the path and round the corner by the damson tree, and then suddenly she whisked into a run towards the paddock and the stables. If I get indigestion it'll just serve me right, she said to herself, but it can't be helped.

CHAPTER 12

Watch Through a Window

For all that Tamzin was so early at the castle, tying Cascade to the gateway thorn tree and creeping in silently, she found the boys were there before her. She saw Roger at once, sitting on a fallen stone near the wall of the keep, and he turned and put a finger to his lips when he heard a small stone roll under her shoes. Tamzin crept on more quietly still, half-stooped as if that would make her less conspicuous to the hoopoes, and crouched down close to Roger.

"Any luck?"

"Sh! Yes, like anything. Watch through that window, into the keep."

Tamzin turned and stared through the broken window-space in the wall of the inner keep. Through it she could see the inside of the opposite wall, but all that she could see there was crumbling stone and flaunting wallflowers. Then suddenly one of the weathered stones detached itself from the wall and Tamzin saw that it was the barred back of a hoopoe. Roger was tugging at her sleeve, but she had seen it as soon as he had. Over the top of the keep the bird flew, out of their sight for a brief half-second and then there it was again, crossing the main area of the castle before it swooped from their view beyond the strong wall.

"They've been coming and going pretty continuously ever since we got here, about twenty minutes ago," whispered Roger. "Meryon's where we were last time, under the outside wall."

"Wow," said Tamzin, "it really does look as if they're nesting, doesn't it? Or do you think it was just eating insects in the wall? I've read them up in Dad's book and it says they do nest in holes, in walls or trees, but hardly ever in this country."

"They've been taking insects *to* the wall," Roger said positively. "There must be two, because one came over, once, almost as soon as the other had gone. They didn't seem to mind my being here at all, though I suppose they must have seen me."

Tamzin was gazing through the window-hole again at the distant wall of the inner keep. "If the nest *is* where the bird was perching, it's really high up."

"Well, that's all to the good," said Roger, "because after we've printed about it in the paper a few people will very likely walk out to have a look. Not many, I suppose, because birds aren't really the sort of thing to excite most Westlingites – even rare birds."

"Sh! Look!" Tamzin clutched his elbow, and again the brilliant stranger was dashing over the wall and across the castle and into the inner keep.

"It did have a worm, or something," she said.

"But I don't think it goes *into* the hole," said Roger, staring intently. "It's so difficult to see, against the stone and so far away. I didn't want to go any closer – into the keep – because of frightening them. Anyway, Meryon and I agreed not to. We were going to change over in half an hour, so when the bird has gone back, we could sneak out."

A moment later the hoopoe glided over the walls again, and probably it settled in the flowering thorn tree because they heard it calling its name, hoopoo-ooe, as one had done before. Running silently on the smooth sheep-bitten grass, Roger and Tamzin went through the castle and out to find Meryon under the wall. To their astonishment they found both Joseph and Rissa as well.

"Sh!" said Rissa, (it seemed that everyone was going to say Sh! now, whenever they came to the castle while the hoopoes were there). "I met Joseph at the farm and we came out together."

"What a hoopoe evening!" said Meryon. "They're putting on the full show. It makes up for those two damp vigils we spent here, seeing nothing but water, doesn't it, Rodge?"

"Ah, that were the wrong time of day," said Joseph. "I knew they was going strong, but I come out here just after sun-up; twice, I did. Going like a shuttle service, they was."

"Look!" said Tamzin under her breath. "That's the hoopoe, still there in the thorn tree; you can see it lifting and dropping its crest. Fancy it not flying away with all of us here – we can't be more than forty feet away."

"They're very tame, if you ask me," said Rissa. "Shockingly so, for a really rare bird."

"But they aren't really rare where they come from," Tamzin said, "in France and Spain and places like that. Oh, *look*! Here comes the other one, while that one's still in the tree! Then there *are* two, just as we thought."

After a moment of silent watching Roger said, "Well, it looks as if we've got the really big scoop every newspaper dreams of, now, though our Westling public won't be the one to appreciate it properly. Anyway, the thing is to keep quiet until the paper comes out, on Monday."

"Only two days, too," said the editor. "Now we've found out all we needed to know about the hoopoes, and only two days to publication, perhaps we ought to be dashing on again. There's lots of business to get through before we can even start last-minute news hunting."

"Unless anyone thinks we ought to make sure about the nest?" Rissa suggested. "I expect Meryon could climb up to it."

Meryon shook his head. "No, I'm dead against it. We don't want to frighten them, do we? And there's quite enough evidence about the nest, with both of them taking food to the same place all the time. Let's leave them in peace."

"I suppose everyone's seen us all in the Local Rag?" Roger asked, standing up and stretching. "I must say I was a bit shaken when I first spotted it – or rather when Dad did and showed it to me – but I don't think it's too bad, really, do you? They must have a simply super reporter gang."

"Oh, I don't know," said Rissa, who was rubbing a dock-leaf on a nettle-stung ankle. "We had nearly a dozen copies buzzing about the district. Probably Doctor Hargreaves' one got into his surgery waiting-room, or Onion Ed wrapped up a reporter's veg. in his, or Mrs Gudgeon showed them hers when they went into the 'Conqueror', as I'm sure reporters do."

"Never mind how they run *their* paper," said Meryon practically, "we've got a lot of work to do on *ours* before Sunday evening."

"It's a bit late, now, to go all the way back to Westling to the stable office," Tamzin said, "but we could go to the farm – where your bikes probably are, anyway – and have a meeting in the stables there, so that we can slap right into reporting and writing-up tomorrow."

They had come round to the castle gateway now and she was unhitching Cascade from the thorn tree.

"I done a bit of news-finding for you," said Joseph, "and two more orders – that's Shepherd Tewmell and a party what comes to us for milk."

"Meryon and I've got nearly a dozen orders between us," Roger said. "It's astonishing, the interest Winklesea people seem to have in Westling news."

"Well, three of them have relations down there, and four were orders in our own families," Meryon pointed out.

"I've got orders for three," said Rissa.

"Oh, terrific," said Tamzin, jumping into her saddle, "and I've got another nine. It really is wonderful, but all the same, think of all the typing! This must bring the circulation up to nearly three dozen, musn't it? Surely there's a better way than typing?"

"There's a duplicator at our school," Roger said, "but I don't think we'd ever get permission to use it."

They were walking on to the farm, now, and Tamzin kept turning her head to see if the hoopoes were flying.

"A bloke I know," said Meryon thoughtfully, "has an ancient printing thing called a hectograph. There isn't much to it – just a shallow tin tray with a sort of printer's jelly in it. You write out one copy of your stuff with a special ink and press it on the jelly; and then all the plain sheets you press on afterwards take the impression."

"I say," said Tamzin enthusiastically, "do you think he'd lend it to us?"

"I expect so; he doesn't use it at all now, I think. He got it at a sale, years ago, for printing handbills about some table rabbits he was breeding, but he doesn't breed them

110

now and so he probably doesn't want any handbills. I'll ask him when I get back tonight, and let you know tomorrow."

"Think of being able just to write out one neat copy, instead of having to type the whole thing at least six times. It would be wonderful," said Tamzin.

Roger opened a sheep-gate and they all filed through. "There is one thing we'd better not lose sight of," he said, "with all this talk of rising circulations and printing gadgets. We've absolutely got to have something to print and circulate, and I'm only hoping some of us have got some news. Meryon and I are a bit handicapped, in mid-week, being so far from the battle area, so to speak, and having spent two whole evenings hunting hoopoes, but we've written up a little thing or two in the feature line."

"I've got a few bits of news," said Tamzin, "nothing really world-shaking, except for the hoopoes, of course. But we've got all of tomorrow for combing the village."

"Next week'll be easier," said Rissa, walking with her hand on Cascade's rump, "because we shan't be needing to spend so much time dashing out to the castle. I only went once, I know, but on two evenings it was pouring, and on the others there just didn't seem to be time after homework. Joseph, you don't know how lucky you are, not going to school."

"I weren't all that lucky when I were a young 'un," said Joseph, as though he were quite grown-up now, "and of course I got to do lessons every morning still, you know that, or the school inspector'd soon be after me. But I allow I am lucky, for all that. It's real nice having a family, and a place of your own."

"Especially a family like the Merrows and a place like Castle Farm," said Tamzin warmly. "What beats me is that the school people never got on your track in all those years

111

you were at sea. I suppose it is all right, our meeting in the stable?" she added, more out of courtesy than doubt, since everyone knew they could do more or less as they liked at the farm.

"You know Mum and Dad as well as I do," said Joseph, with his faint, shy smile.

"All right, then. What we want to do is list the news and feature items we've already got for Number Two, and see if we can work up any more features. And then make a full list of names and addresses of new subscribers. Oh, I've got three entries for the competition, Rodge! One from Mrs Briggs (I persuaded her when she brought the washing round, the other evening), and one from Doctor Hargreaves (he had to adapt the title to 'Why I Would Like to Live in Westling'), and one from Mrs Clench, of all people."

"Have you got them with you?" Roger asked with interest.

Tamzin shook her head. "I don't carry the office's vital papers about the Marsh with me." She had broken a small branch from a ditchside willow and was using it to waft the flies from Cascade's head.

"Who're we going to get to do the judging?" Meryon asked.

As no one had any ideas, Tamzin said, "I think we could try all of us reading them, and then voting among ourselves. But really Mrs Clench's is easily the best of this lot, even better than Doctor Hargreaves', though his is funnier. But hers is all about how nice it is to be caretakers of a village Sailors' Institute, and watching the men play billiards there in the evenings, and listening on wild nights for the lifeboat going out to bring back shipwrecked sailors for her and Mr Clench to look after in the dormitory."

"I can't see her wanting three natty gent's handkies," said Meryon, "all the same."

"No," said Tamzin, "but her Albert would. And that'd please her more than three for herself. I think I'll put Cascade in the stable, Joseph, and not in the orchard with Siani, because it's so hot and the flies are so awful. It'll be nice having him at the meeting, too."

"We can rest our notebooks on him," said Roger, "and prop our weary limbs."

But Tamzin didn't answer him, as she slipped from the saddle at the farm gate and looked with pleasure at the thatch-roofed farmhouse with its plume of smoke, and the brown hens luxuriously dusting themselves outside the door.

CHAPTER 13

Life's Disasters

On the Saturday morning, after she had helped her mother in the house for half an hour or so because of its not being one of Mrs Brigg's mornings, Tamzin rushed round to the "William the Conqueror" to see if Mrs Gudgeon had finished with last week's issue of the *Westling News* and, if so, whether she could spare it for Harbour Farm.

Smiling Morn's solid garden fence stood up, high and forbidding, at the corner where the Main Street swung round to the Point and the Hard and the Harbour, and it was just here that Tamzin nearly fell a victim to the pace of British roads. There wasn't very much excuse for her because she had heard the engine of Jim Decks' wheelchair perfectly well as she went dashing round the corner, but unfortunately she had again supposed that it was only Onion Ed's Silver Bullet, which would never have reached more than a walking pace on that treacherous, shingly surface.

There was an awful muddled moment in which Tamzin suddenly saw what was coming, and how fast and how close, and she instinctively threw out her hands and jumped sideways. She wasn't to know that Jim, swerving his wheelchair to avoid her, would choose the same direction.

The first thing she really clearly knew was that she was, incredibly, somehow sitting astride the front of the wheelchair, facing backwards and rushing round the remainder of the tricky corner on two of the wheelchair's three wheels. Only about twelve inches from her eyes was the agitated face of the ferryman, his wild beard blowing and hair whipping up under the battered peaked cap that Tamzin had knocked sideways. He was making a noise that sounded like "pop-pop-pop" (and so was the engine, only not so loud), but luckily Tamzin soon realised that this noise really meant that she was in the way of the brake and he hadn't got the anchor on board. This was just as well, as they were by now swerving dangerously up the village street, old Jim's visibility being limited by his sudden and unexpected passenger. Tamzin managed to reach the brake, and the wheelchair skidded to a lurching stop which tossed Tamzin right into Smiling Morn's open shop doorway. Scrambling to her feet among the staring customers, she went straight out again to see if Jim was all right, with Smiling Morn's sorrowful voice following after her: "What a way to come into anyone's shop – and not buying anything, either . . ."

For about five minutes Tamzin and Jim each made sure that the other was all right and that the wheelchair was all right, and each very unselfishly said that the fault was all theirs, though thinking that the other could have been a lot more careful; and then, seeing that a crowd was beginning to gather, old Jim let in his clutch and went on his precarious way, swooping erratically up through the village with his crutches, which Tamzin was certain he would never use, stuck up dramatically beside him.

Being able now to turn her attention to the little cluster of villagers round her, Tamzin realised with embarrassment that she was being dusted down by Mrs Smeed and offered a drink of water by plump little Mrs Goldeye who had rushed out from the back of the shop on hearing sounds of calamity, for she loved a nice little disaster.

"Oh, thanks awfully – it's very kind of you, but really I'm quite all right," Tamzin said as firmly as she could. "I'm rather in a hurry, so I'll just dash off again, now, if you don't mind." And, before anyone could make a proper answer, she dashed.

The "William the Conqueror" wasn't open yet, because of the earliness of the hour, but Tamzin found Mrs Gudgeon cleaning windows round at the back, and explained about the secondhand paper she was needing.

"Well, you're welcome to it, dearie – what there is of it," Mrs Gudgeon said, wringing out her wash-leather: "but the fact is, so many folks has been reading it, see, when they come in of an evening, that it isn't what it was. Real popular that paper been, and I tell no lie."

Pondering on this as Mrs Gudeon was indoors finding the copy, Tamzin wondered whether selling a paper to a village inn, where numbers of people (too many, by the sound of things) could read it at leisure and for nothing, was really good business. But you couldn't actually *refuse* to sell a copy to anyone, especially after having pleaded with them to take it, she decided.

The paper wasn't in too bad condition, Tamzin was pleased to see when Mrs Gudgeon brought it – all the pages were there and all were more or less readable and only one corner was torn off. She raced home with it cheerfully, slowing down with sudden caution at Smiling Morn's corner, but all that she met round the other side of it was Dickon walking carefully Point-wards with a jar of dusty-looking potato leaves clutched in both hands.

116

Rissa, Meryon and Roger were all in the stable loft office when she got there, leaning over the goat-bench and examining something laid on it.

"Meryon's got the hectograph thing," Rissa called, hearing Tamzin's shoes on the ladder. "Come and look!"

"Oh fantastic!" Tamzin climbed out on to the floor and dashed across it. "Oh, there isn't much to it, is there? Only a trayful of jelly stuff."

"What's wrong with that?" asked Meryon. "You don't want a roomful of knobs and keys and wheels and things if a simple tray will do the job as well. We'll experiment with it this afternoon, or this evening if there isn't time before. But just now, if we're going to whip up any news at all to experiment with, we ought to be hot on the trail."

"Yes, in a minute," said Tamzin, "but here you behold the survivor of an honest-to-goodness road accident. I've just been snatched up and carried a full ten yards on Jim's chair – just as if it were a cow-catcher. That thing really can go. It'll be a wonder if anyone much is left alive in Westling if he goes on at this rate – him included."

"I bet you were dashing round Smiling Morn's corner and not looking," said Rissa. "Anyway, I dare say we can work it up a bit for the paper. 'Vicar's Daughter Carried off on Invalid Chair' ought to go down quite well."

"If anyone writes it up, I'm going to, because it was me it happened to," said Tamzin.

"All right, but later on," said their editor. "Just now it's sleuthing for news, and if we don't get on the road in five minutes it just won't be worth going at all."

Without their usual discussions and arguments they split up quickly into two reporting parties, each covering one half of the village and all to meet in the loft again about midday. Tamzin, who had Meryon with her this time, said they would do the west half of the village, though it was the dullest, not having the river and the harbour, because Harbour Farm was in that half and she had to go there anyhow.

"I don't know who's running the ferry this morning," she said, pushing a hand in her jeans pocket to make sure her note book was there, "with old Jim out in his wheelchair. You could find that out, Rodge and Rissa. Come on, Meryon, we can climb over the wall, it's much quicker."

On the way to the farm, which lay at the extreme westerly edge of the village, Tamzin told Meryon about the Deeproses' hen that was mothering two orphan kittens. "I expect they'd let us see it, if we asked," she said. "I'd love to, and I suppose we really ought if we're going to put it in the paper, but there wasn't time when I was there before."

They were just going round to the back door of the farmhouse when they heard sounds of a commotion in the farmyard, and stopped and stared at one another, and then they were both running round the buildings towards the source of the disturbance. At the farmyard gate Mrs and Miss Deeprose stood gazing in consternation into the yard where the big Friesian bull was standing pawing and snorting with·the door of his bull-pen open behind him.

"He broke loose," Mrs Deeprose said to Tamzin in a voice that was trying determinedly not to be shaky. "It isn't a proper bull-pen, and I was always afraid of this."

"He can't get out of the yard, I think," said Miss Deeprose, whose hands were gripping tightly on the gate-top, "but he's been loose in there for more than an hour, now. They've tried to drive him back in, but he just goes straight at anyone that sets foot in there, and nobody can get at any of the buildings. The milk is in the dairy, there – the milk lorry had to go without it – and there's a

118

cow calving in the shed, and Bert can't get at the food-store or the tractor. And there's the trailer in the middle of the yard, that they'll be wanting in the hayfield."

"Charlie just managed to get into the calf-shed," said his mother, looking across to the line of buildings down the right-hand side of the yard where the choir master could be seen in a shadowed doorway, "and now he's stuck there, too. I don't know what will be the end of it . . ." she paused for a moment, trying not to think of it, "but it's a valuable bull. It'd be a blow to lose it, but worse to lose our Charlie or Bert."

At that moment the wind blew the bull-pen door shut, and it looked to Tamzin as if that was that, since the bull could now not possibly get back into his place of his own accord. He swung round at the sudden slamming noise, and Charlie snatched the opportunity to slip out of the calf-shed again and dash across the corner of the yard to the food-store. He only just got the door shut behind him as the bull came sliding to a stop on the threshold, steaming and grumbling. Mrs Deeprose put her hands up over her eyes, and Meryon touched her shoulder reassuringly.

"He's all right. He's in there, Mrs Deeprose."

Bert, looking on from the stackyard over the opposite wall, understood his employer's manœuvre and now began to call the bull: "Come on, Sultan, old fellow: come on here!"

The bull lifted his head and veered round, trotting over arrogantly like a fighting bull in an arena. The door of the food-store cracked open quietly and Charlie came out with a bucket of dairy nuts and oats, such as Sultan liked above anything else. He was moving cautiously down the edge of the yard towards Sultan's bull-pen, lifting up handfuls of feed and dropping them back enticingly, as Rissa some-

119

times did when catching Siani, but Sultan was past being enticed with dainty morsels. He turned his head and looked, and saw the nuts and oats and saw Charlie, and it was Charlie that he wanted. There was no getting back to the food-store this time. Charlie dropped his bucket and leaped on to the empty trailer that was so luckily waiting to go out to the field again when this sudden crisis was over.

"Oh, my lord!" said Mrs Deeprose, feeling that she could neither look nor look away.

"He's all right now, Mother," said her daughter, but the bull began to rock the trailer, and with such devilish power and purpose that it looked as if he would soon succeed in heaving it over.

Almost together, Bert and Meryon now climbed into the farmyard from their opposite sides, and Tamzin's eyes opened wide in fearful apprehension. This was really the Spanish bullring in front of her eyes, transported to a peaceful Sussex farmyard: there was the cornered matador up on the trailer, and there were the toreros running in to create a diversion.

The big bull, sleek in his smooth summer coat, was baffled by this sudden development of alternative victims. He half-turned from the trailer, pawing and swinging his heavy head, blowing on the ground; and then the spilled oat-grains blew up under his nose so that he caught the sweet smell of them. Suddenly he decided to shelve his problems for a while in a break for refreshment. His big, shining nose-ring tapped on the ground as he licked and snuffled the feed. Meryon, standing at flight-point in the yard, looked at it with a kind of fascination, and then saw out of the corner of his eye a pitchfork lying along the empty trailer – four pitchforks – and one within arm's reach if he made a single careful sidestep.

Tamzin, watching him in a state of frozen horror, was convinced that he was going to attack the bull with the pitchfork, so that when she saw him slowly leaning forward with it, like a man spearing eels, until he had pinned the bull's nose-ring down to the ground with a prong of it, she could hardly prevent herself from shouting her relief and astonishment, and then shouting again because of the urgency of someone quickly doing something else about it. But someone was. Already, while Sultan was stamping and grumbling and realising just what had happened to him in his single off-guard moment, Charlie and Bert were racing to get the chains and pole that usually controlled him. For a minute Meryon stood there, holding on to the dug-in pitchfork, and only a single prong of it through the bull's ring was between him and all that an angry bull could do to him.

Charlie and Bert came tearing back with the bull-tackle, and all in a moment the chains and pole were clipped on, and the pitchfork was back on the trailer, and Bert was leading Sultan back to his box. Mrs Deeprose and her daughter were clasping each other in their anxiety and relief, and Tamzin was standing on the bottom bar of the gate and leaning over saying ridiculously and inconsequently, "Oh goodness! I just – however did you – I was afraid he——" and things like that.

Charlie and Bert rammed the bolts home on Sultan's door, and Charlie shut the top door, too, to keep him quiet until they had done something about reinforcing those bolts. And then, just as if nothing extraordinary had happened at all, Charlie said, "Well now, Bert, you'd better fix those bolts and have a look at Rosie, and get the calves hayed up, and then we'll take the tractor and trailer up to the seven-acre and carry on loading." He turned to Meryon and said with the embarrassed grin men often have

121

for bravery and presence of mind, "Reckon you've got a career in Spain waiting for you feller! Any time you want a reference, just apply to me."

Meryon grinned back. "I'd have been up on the trailer with you, like a shot, if he'd so much as taken a look at me," he admitted a little sheepishly, "but he was only thinking of his grub."

"Like Roger," said Tamzin, laughing shakily.

"Now you both come in and have some elevenses," said Mrs Deeprose, who was almost her usual self again, but Tamzin thanked her and refused politely. "We'd love to, but we're really pushed for time. We've got almost all the work on Monday's paper to do yet. Really, we only came to bring you this last-week's edition, and to ask if we could see the hen that mothers the orphan kittens."

"And to look for news," said Meryon, grinning again.

"Well, seemingly," said Bert, who was pouring diesel oil into the tractor, "you been and got that, ole young'uns!"

"I say," said Tamzin, suddenly thinking of it, "so we have! What a wonderful headline for the paper! I was so busy being terrified and all that, I never thought about the news aspect."

"That's the best of being in the newspaper line," said Meryon. "All life's worst disasters can be turned to good purpose, and the worse they are the more useful from the news point of view."

"I know," said Tamzin, "but you only think of that afterwards - it doesn't make the disaster any less terrifying while it's happening. Or not to me."

CHAPTER 14

It Ought to be Dead Easy

No other news collected that morning was to be compared, for sheer drama, with the bull incident at Harbour Farm. Meryon and Tamzin picked up a few small items, such as the measles now spreading into Westling from Dunsmere where it had started the week before, and the mackerel season beginning well with big shoals in the Bay, and (from Mrs Beatup, whom they found making a large fish pudding in her kitchen) how Mrs Galley had locked Hookey out all night when he came home drunk, and how Miss Pemble was in such a fix owing to having trodden on her false teeth and not having any spare ones, and how old Annie Upjohn – sister of Thomas – went up to London in a railway train on Monday for the very first time in her life, and that was only to a funeral, even then.

"Mrs Beatup's news isn't really as good as I thought it would be," Meryon said as they walked back down the village street. "I don't think we dare put in the bit about Hookey, do you? So soon after putting in about his fight with Walter? He'd begin to think we were picking on him."

"Never mind," said Tamzin, "the bull news is good enough to make up for a lot of waffle, and we've got the hoopoes."

"Pity we've all had measles," said Meryon, "when it's galloping over the river the way it is now. We could all have done with a good June holiday with so much to do on the paper."

Up in the loft they found Roger and Rissa home before them. Tamzin's father was sitting with them on the goat-bench and they were all working absorbedly at a problem Tamzin knew of old (though she had never met anyone who knew the answer) concerning the taking of gas, water and electricity from three works to three houses without crossing any lines or pipes.

"Oh, that thing," said Tamzin, coming across the floor. "It can't be done."

"It can," said Roger. "I knew a bloke, once, who could do it. In fact, I saw him."

"Well, how did he do it then?"

"I don't remember; it was ages ago. But I know he did."

"Oh! You've been drawing all over our sermon paper!" said Tamzin, aghast.

"Only four pieces," said her father apologetically. "I'll find you four more. You know, you could put this problem in your paper, with a prize for the first correct entry. I didn't really come to suggest that, but you could."

"I suppose we could," said Meryon, squatting on the floor. "It's a good idea."

"Especially as no one's likely to get it right," said Rissa, "because we're really short of prizes."

Mr Grey put all the scribbled-on pages neatly together, with a large pebble that Roger was using as a paperweight on top. "I don't think you need worry about that – for this week, at any rate. I could give you a box of green writing paper that someone sent me last Christmas; neither Gwen nor I like it very much. But what I really came up for was to see if you would put in an advertisement for me."

"Oh, yes, certainly sir," said Roger, very businesslike, though since so many people were sitting on his desk he couldn't function at it. "Have you got it drafted out, or would you like us to do that?"

"I could dictate it," said the vicar. "It isn't very long."

"Ready," said Roger, reaching for his pencil from under Rissa's hand.

" 'We don't go to God's House,' " said the vicar slowly, " 'because we are good, but because we are bad. If any of us were perfect, we shouldn't need to go. Are you good enough to stay at home? I know I'm not.' And then put, Richard Grey."

"Wow, Mrs One-Who-Knows will goggle at that," said Tamzin.

"She may never see it," said the vicar. "The great thing is to encourage a few who may have been thinking they weren't really good enough to come. Now, here's the money – payment with order – and I must be dashing off: I have to see Mr Goldeye before lunch."

"Nothing wrong, I hope?" asked Roger, after the vicar had sunk out of sight down the ladder.

Tamzin shook her head. "I shouldn't think so. It's just that he's Vicar's Warden. But listen! We've got some really terrifically gorgeous news for the paper. Meryon's just caught an escaped bull. We couldn't tell you before because of wanting it to be news for Dad when he reads it in the paper."

"Listen to me, young woman," said Meryon firmly, taking her by the wrists, "I didn't catch a bull, and I won't have you say I did, or even hint at such a thing in the paper." He put her two hands into her jean pockets for her, sat her down on a corner of the goat-bench and said,

"Now you sit there quietly and I'll tell them."

Meryon's tale was exciting enough until he came to Charlie's being chased up on to the trailer, but after that Tamzin thought it sagged shockingly.

"Well, Bert and I both thought we couldn't leave Charlie to his fate, so we tried to attract the bull's notice – with shouting and all that, you know——"

"They rushed into the yard," began Tamzin, but Meryon put a large brown hand over her mouth and held it there.

"But just about then he, – the bull – got wind of the grub Charlie had upset when he was leaping for the trailer, and after that everything was dead easy because he was so busy gobbling it that I put a hayfork through his ring – that's what she was so thrilled about," he added, "and then Bert and Charlie came dashing up with cables and warps and poles and things, and the old boy walked back into his box as mild as a sheep. And Tamzin and I went off and looked at a hen with two kittens."

"Kittens!" said Rissa. "It all sounds a bit far-fetched to me."

"All right, let them think it was easy if you like," Tamzin said, roused and ruffled, "I don't care. We didn't have much else in the news line," she told the others. "I hope you did – though we aren't badly off really, for this edition, are we?"

"We went round to see how Jim was getting on," Rissa said, "and I give you fifty thousand guesses who was running the ferry for him."

"Hookey Galley, fifty thousand times," said Tamzin, since he seemed the most unlikely and unhelpful person she could think of.

"Mrs Beatup, Gypsophila Lillycrop, Onion Ed, Smiling Morn," said Meryon, adding his unlikely selection.

"All wrong," said Roger. "It was old Jim's father."

Tamzin and Meryon stared at him for a long disbelieving minute, and then Tamzin said, "It couldn't be. He's much too old to have a father."

"Everyone's got a father," argued Rissa. "It's just that old Jim's hasn't died yet, and you thought he must have. Long life runs in their family."

"But – where's he been all this time? And what does he look like?" It didn't seem possible to Tamzin that she could have known Jim and Westling all these years and still not have known this thing about them.

"Young Jimmy told us he lives with Jim's Aunt Ada out at Hythe," said Roger. "What does he look like? Well, like a – like a——"

"Like Abraham and Isaac and all the prophets," said Rissa. "But astonishingly active."

"He must be at least ninety," said Tamzin, marvelling. "What's he called?"

"Old Jim," said Roger.

"No! I say, how awfully muddling. I wonder what Jim's – our Jim's – 'Stacia thinks? I suppose old Jim – Jim's father – is staying there."

"Yes, for a little time, while Aunt Ada has an operation for gallstones, Jimmy says. It was really funny, because every time we asked old Jim anything, such as would he like us to help with the ferry, or was he going to apply to take a driving test now, he said, 'I'll have to see what Dad says'."

Tamzin grinned and Meryon gave a sudden guffaw. "The old fraud, he's putting it on," he said.

"Of course, no one really knows how old Jim is," said Tamzin, "he could be only about seventy, I suppose, or even less, and his father not more than ninety. You do

127

sometimes hear of people still being awfully nimble at ninety. There was some old man of nearly a hundred who still walked four miles a day."

"Well, after all that – which really is quite good news, I think," went on Roger, "we chased about all over the harbour and up and down the river, but we didn't see anything much except a few boats going out and Johnny Beatup fishing for eels, and Dickon baiting Jerusalem with potato leaves."

"And those day-trippers with the dinghy," reminded Rissa.

"Oh yes, they were terrifically funny, but not really news, I suppose. They'd hired a sailing dinghy from the Tomsetts and honestly they spent the whole morning drifting backwards and forwards across the river, and being fended off by all the other boats in the harbour."

"They forgot to lower their centreboard," said Rissa, grinning. "Sails and sheets trailing in the water – you never saw such a muddle. In the end they lost the tide and never went out at all."

"Oh well, perhaps they were good at golf, or painting, or something," said Tamzin, who was always willing to think the best of anyone if she could. "Never mind, we must build up this week's edition on the hoopoes – they're really the top news – and the bull; and then have our smaller items mixed with any features we can dredge up. I'm sure it's better to mix them up a bit than to have news and features separate, the way we did last week." She glanced into her notebook. "We've got another nice bit about Jim's chair – he won't mind – and there's the Colorado, and the Deeproses' hen, and Mrs Merrow's egg, and perhaps Miss Pemble's teeth – though I'm not sure about that; we'd have to be careful how we put it – and Annie Upjohn going to

London, and we might put in a Farming Note on the state of the haying."

"There's the measles, and Joseph's news about the coin they dug up," reminded Meryon, "and Rodge and I've both got feature articles. Mine's a thing about First Aid and Roger's is on cricket."

"The one thing proper newspapers have better than us is illustrations," said the editor. "I suppose our pin drawings were all right in their way, but they're an awful sweat to do so many times. That ought to be dead easy with the hectograph, though," he added, "oughtn't it, Meryon? One drawing, and peel it off as often as we like."

"It sounds marvellous," said Tamzin.

But in fact that wasn't at all what they thought when they really got started on it in the office after lunch.

"The bloke left it all ready to use," Meryon said, "but when we've printed this issue on it we'll have to melt the jelly down again and re-set it ready for next week. It's the only way to get the ink impression off. This is the ink," he explained, lifting a bottle of it out of a little box.

"Ugh! Violet," said Rissa. "I'm not going to be a reporter to a violet newspaper."

"You are," said Meryon, "you haven't any choice, except not being a reporter at all, because this is the proper ink for a hectograph."

"Never mind," said Roger, "it makes us different from other newspapers."

"Lots of things do that," said Rissa.

"I think the tray will take all our four sheets," said Meryon, trying them.

"But what about the reverse sides?" Rissa asked practically.

"I never thought of that! Well, we'll just have to melt the

stuff down and do them after the first four. What a nuisance. I wonder if it takes long to set?"

"I expect we'll soon find out," said Roger, "and the sooner we get started on the first lot, the better it'll be for the second lot if it does take a long time to set."

Each member of the staff was given one page to write out in the violet ink and, as all were being done at once and at the same goat-bench, there was a certain amount of wrangling and muddle. Everything had first to be roughed out in ordinary pencil, so that they could see exactly what was going on each page, and then the final copies had to be done in perfect neatness.

"'Our ferry is so popular'," Tamzin was saying as she wrote, "'that even germs are using it. Measles has now arrived from Dunsford'."

"Shut up," said Rissa crossly. "If we all said everything aloud as we wrote it the place would sound like Waterloo Station. How do you spell 'inhabitant'? ant or ent?"

"Ant," said Meryon. "How do you spell hoopoes?"

Tamzin told him, remembering it from the bird book.

"And the last syllable is like canoe or lasso for pronouncing. I say, do give them really banner headlines, Meryon – THE FANTASTIC STRANGERS –" she wrote it in the air in large capitals. "They're our big scoop."

"And the Colorado," Rissa said. "That was a fantastic stranger, too."

"Three advertisements," said Roger. "That's good going," but Tamzin explained about not asking Jim to pay for his. "I had thought of getting Mrs Gudgeon to put one in," she said, "but everyone knows about the 'Conqueror' already."

"I do think this purple ink looks awful," said Rissa.

"It'll be paler when we print it off, of course," said

Meryon, and Rissa said she thought that would be worse, because mauve was worse than purple.

When the exciting moment came of pressing the inked pages face down on the hard-set jelly, it was well on in the afternoon. The suspense of wondering whether there would really be an impression when the pages were peeled off was quite dreadful, but they need not have worried – there was.

"It's all back to front," said Tamzin, gazing at it, "like mirror writing."

"It has to be, idiot," said Rissa, "so that it prints off properly on to the paper."

"Now for the blank sheets," said Roger, fetching them from the orange-box. "Here you are, Meryon."

For another few minutes the suspense returned in full as Meryon pressed the first four blank sheets on to the jelly.

"There, I should think that would do. Now let's have a look."

One after the other the sheets came peeling off, to be studied in silence by the editor and staff.

"Well, you can read it," said Rissa. "I think it's rather disappointing. It isn't only that awful fainting mauve colour, and the washiness, but our handwritings aren't half as professional-looking as the typing was."

"The drawings came out all right," said Roger, who had done the gas, water and elecricity puzzle, with six small drawn squares only to it.

"Do you think so?" asked Tamzin doubtfully. She had drawn a thumbnail sketch of the hoopoes flying, and didn't think that pale purple suited them.

"Oh well," said Rissa, "if it doesn't come out any paler as we go on . . . I suppose it is much less trouble than the typing, though we didn't have to do a neat handwritten copy first, for that."

But it did come out paler as they went on. By the time the last few copies had been peeled off, it was extremely difficult to read them at all, and a general feeling of disappointment prevailed in the office.

"And now we've got to melt the stuff down and wait for it to set before we can do the next lot," sighed Tamzin. "What a good thing it's a Saturday, and Mrs Briggs not here. I'm sure she'd never let us melt a sinister-looking jelly like that in any cooking saucepan. But Mother won't mind."

"We've still got to write out the neat, beastly violet copies of the last four pages," said Rissa, "while it sets."

But they had written those out – and one of them twice because of Roger accidentally jogging Tamzin's arm while she was writing – and had tea in the vicarage garden, and watered the ponies, and spent half an hour helping Dickon to look for Jerusalem before the jelly had set again.

"It's because of the summer and hot weather," Meryon explained.

But when it really had set, Tamzin nearly cried at the sight of it. "Look! All ribbed, like corrugated cardboard! And we put it on a flat place, and everything."

"It looks like Dunsmere Sands when the wind's been racing over them," said Rissa disgustedly.

"But there hasn't been any wind up here!" Tamzin wailed.

"The bloke did say it was a bit tricky to set level," Meryon admitted. "I wonder what we did wrong?"

"We'd have done much better to stick to the typing," said Rissa positively.

"I think we'd better melt it down and have another try," said the editor. "After all, we've got half the edition printed on it, now."

132

"It'll take all night to set," said Rissa, "and then I bet you my bust pencil it'll come out like a switchback again."

"There is a least one bright aspect," said Meryon. "We can all go swimming, whereas if it had set properly we'd all be toiling at printing and assembling till time to go home. The tide's up beautifully high now – high enough to swim in the harbour."

"Dad doesn't much like us working on the paper on a Sunday," said Tamzin doubtfully, but very much tempted by the thought of blue-green, gliding water, cool and lovely after the heat and concentration of the office, "but perhaps he'd overlook it just once. I don't know about all of you, but next week I'm in favour of going back to typing, whatever the struggle."

"Well, we'll see," said Meryon. "Perhaps I'll think of something else."

CHAPTER 15

The Scoop

Sunday was the sort of day the soonest forgotten the better. There was, of course, church in the morning for Tamzin, who was in the choir as usual, under the boat-shaped, round-ended roof that was so right for a fishing village church. Rissa went with her mother to St. Mary's, Dunsford, which is the finest church in all Sussex excepting only Chichester Cathedral, standing up on the crown of its hill above all the old town, where it has stood since the earliest days of Dunsford's wild history. Roger was at Winklesea, a church old and bloodstained too: the town still talked of the dark day in the third Edward's reign when three thousand Norman raiders surprised the citizens during Mass, dragging them from their worship with a very great slaughter, so that a nearby street is still called Dead Man's Lane. But Meryon was not at church this morning, being occupied with discovering all that could be discovered about printing a small village newspaper.

It wasn't the morning that was so terrible, but the rest of the day – blue and gold and lovely though it was – because the whole of it was spent struggling in the office with the hectograph, and assembling the "fainting mauve" pages that it had reluctantly brought forth. When all was finished the result was so poor that Tamzin and Meryon might well have stayed up all night doing the whole thing again on the vicar's typewriter, if they had thought such a thing might ever be allowed.

Late in the evening, sitting at the goat-bench writing on each copy the name of the subscriber who had ordered it, Tamzin screwed up her eyes in the failing light from the loft window and sighed deeply. Rissa had already left for home, and Meryon and Roger would soon be following, taking with them the copies ordered for Winklesea and district.

"We'll just have to tell everyone it was a printing experiment," Roger said, combing his hair by guess and feel for the journey home, "and that next week we'll be back to typing."

"Typing such a lot of copies – even with five carbons – will be abso-bally-lutely awful," said Tamzin, "but as far as I'm concerned, Meryon, you can take the darned hectograph back with you tonight. I mean, if we can't turn out a better-looking paper than this it would be as well not to turn one out at all."

"I did hope," said Meryon, "to be able to track down a proper duplicator this morning, but it was no good. The only one I could find belongs to a club, and the secretary pointed out that it would be very difficult – impossible, he said – to arrange for lending or hiring club property. Anyway, I did think of one thing, which was whether they would do the printing for us."

"But they would have to charge something, even if it wasn't very much," said Tamzin, "and we need every penny for Jim's fund. Even at the rate we're going, it'll take an awful long time to pay off the damages."

"It'll take even longer," said Roger sensibly, "if we have to keep our circulation down because of you and Meryon not being able to type more than, say, three dozen copies. We've got nearly three dozen ordered this week, already. Well, we're not going to be content with that, are we? We want circs. of six dozen, eight dozen, and more, if the thing's going to be any good at all."

"I'll see what I can find out," Meryon promised. "Perhaps, if they will do them, they won't charge very much. We can only ask."

"Here are your copies," Tamzin said, handing them over, "all done at last. It's nearly nine o'clock already, and no swimming, no riding, no outdoors of any kind. As far as we were concerned the sun need never have been shining at all today."

Meryon grinned at her cheerfully, tucking the bundle of violet-inked papers under his arm. "Cheer up, old young 'un! The sun will shine again. And even if you don't like the look of the *Westling News*, Number Two, doesn't it contain the scoop of the century?"

In a sense, perhaps it did – certainly the scoop of Westling's year, though it was a day or two before anyone connected with the paper realised this. Tamzin, cycling home on the Monday across a faintly hazy Marsh on which the light was playing its old tricks with shape and size and distance, noticed a man's tall figure walking out across the grazings towards Cloudesley Castle, and somehow he didn't look like any of the shepherds that she knew. She stared at him so long and hard as she cycled over the stony, humpy road, that she finally skidded in a pothole and fell off into the middle of the road, giving herself a bad graze on her knee and a worse one on the palm of her left hand. But she had pretty certainly identified the walker as Hookey Galley. Yes, it was definitely Hookey, without doubt. No one else walked quite like that, with knees so curiously jerky as if they were worked by something mechanical.

Pedalling on homeward, Tamzin wondered what Hookey could be doing. He was a strange man, born, it seemed, without any ordinary sense of honour and values. If anyone, Tamzin pondered, could be called a snake in Westling's grass, it was Hookey Galley. It was everyone's natural reaction, if they saw him doing anything unusual, to wonder what he was up to, and Tamzin was wondering this all the way home. On the surface of things, he had probably read about the hoopoes in the morning's *Westling News*, which he could easily have picked up at the "Conqueror" and was innocently going to have a look. But Hookey was not interested in birds, except the edible kind, and never went for walks across the Marsh, unless for a definite (and profitable) purpose, and above all, whatever else he was, he was hardly ever innocent.

Considering all these aspects, Tamzin was uneasy, but not extremely so. The hoopoes' nest was very high and difficult to reach, and it didn't seem likely that anyone could possibly want to hurt them . . . but all the same, she decided to ride out in the evening, after tea, and make sure that they were all right.

Mrs Grey, weeding in the garden while the kettle boiled, greeted her daughter on the path.

"Darling! You look tired – and what have you done to your knee?"

"It's my hand as well." She held it out. "I fell off my bike, believe it or not. Silly of me, really, but I was looking at Hookey Galley walking out towards the castle, and wondering what he was up to."

"You needn't really have wondered. I expect he was only up to what several other people have been up to, all day – going out to look at your hoopoes. My word, you certainly

137

stirred up some interest there, Tamzin! I'd never have believed our stolid Westlingites would have been so interested in a bird – even such a rare one as a hoopoe."

"Oh," said Tamzin, half-pleased because their scoop seemed really to have come off, and half-uneasy for the peace and quiet of the hoopoes. "But I'd never have thought Hookey——"

"Oh, the most unlikely people have been going out," said her mother, dropping her trowel into the weeding-trug. "Come in and I'll do your hand and knee, and we can talk about it then."

In the kitchen, warm with the hot stove and the hot June sun through the wide open window, Tamzin sat with her leg stretched out while her mother dabbed with antiseptic water and told how she had three times directed strangers to the castle, people who had inquired at the door of the shortest way there, having heard the news of the hoopoes in the "Conqueror", or at the post office or the ferry.

"I didn't really like telling them," she admitted, "because I'm sure it's better for the birds to be left alone, but they'd have got there somehow in any case, since anyone can see the castle for miles and miles around. It was only the shortest way they wanted to know. And of course I did ask them particularly not to go too near or disturb the birds in any way, and they all seemed to understand and agree about that. Then there were all kinds of people from the village going out, even Mrs Goldeye and Mrs Venus, who probably haven't walked to the castle for fifteen years. . . . Now your hand, Tamzin – how difficult this grit is to get out."

Tamzin put her hand cautiously into the hot milky water and withdrew it again quickly. "Ouch! it really does sting. Can you do it while I just hold it over the water? Yes, like that." She winced as the swab touched the grazed area. "Trippers: I don't know what to think of that. I never thought of trippers and visitors going out, or even that they'd hear about the birds; and none of us thought many people in the village would, somehow. We knew it was a terrific scoop of news really, of course, but we didn't think the village would take it that way. You know how unmoved everyone usually is, even about things like floods and disasters. . . . I do hope the hoopoes didn't mind."

"So do I," said Mrs Grey, squeezing out her cotton-wool swab and taking a fresh one. "Honestly, my pet, I do wonder if you did wisely in putting such a thing into the paper. Anyway, if Richard and I had known about it, I think we'd both have advised against it. I know I would. But never mind, it's too late now. All we can hope is that their admiring public don't disturb them too badly."

Tamzin frowned perplexedly. "We didn't tell you – or anyone else except Joseph – because we wanted it to be proper news when you got your paper."

She looked so worried that her mother said consolingly, "I shouldn't worry. Perhaps after today, when the novelty has worn off a bit, people will leave them alone. There, that's the best I can do with those grazes. I haven't put tea in the garden today, because the wind seemed so fresh, but Dickie and I pushed the table into the sitting-room window, and we've got a bowl – a very small bowl – of the very first strawberries."

"Oh, my!" Tamzin grinned appreciatively at her and decided to shelve her worry about the hoopoes until after tea, so that nothing could possibly come between her and the heaven of June's first strawberries.

After tea the whole vicarage family went out to see the hoopoes, Tamzin and Dickon riding ahead on Cascade and

Banner, and Mr and Mrs Grey walking after them, he with his binoculars and pocket bird book, and she with a little notice that she and Tamzin had drafted out and painted on a piece of old rabbit-hutch board:

PLEASE DO NOT DISTURB THE HOOPOES.
PLEASE, PLEASE KEEP WELL AWAY.

"Three pleases on one notice," Mrs Grey had said, wiping her paintbrush, "That ought to do the trick. It's amazing how far a little politeness goes."

"If the noticeboard was bigger," Tamzin said, "we could've put much more," but her mother said that people never read long notices, it was better to keep them compact, and she probably knew, as a parson's wife with long experience of parish notice-writing.

It was perfectly plain to see, from quite a distance away, that several people were still standing and walking about near the castle, and Tamzin hurried Cascade on because she began to feel so anxious for the hoopoes.

"We're leaving Mother and Dad behind," Dickon said, letting Banner break into a canter behind her.

"I don't think they'll mind; they were a good way back anyhow, and they know how anxious I am to make sure the birds are still all right. We can all walk home together," she added.

A few yards from the castle they tied the ponies to a post-and-rail sheep-fence, not liking to add to the population by tying them up to the tree by the gateway.

"At least six people there," Tamzin was saying as she let out Cascade's girths and ran his irons up the leathers, "and why do they have to talk so loudly? Listen to that woman laughing!" She was shocked and very anxious. "Come on,

Dicky! Oh dear, I do hope they're all right."

"Well, it was you that started it," said Dickon. "If you hadn't put about it in your paper, nobody would've been there at all."

"I never thought——" began Tamzin, and then, "Oh, be *quiet*; how on earth could I know? Besides, Mrs Beatup would have spread it around. Have you slackened his girths? All right, then, come on."

Only two of the people at the castle were Westling people, and neither of them was Hookey, who it seemed, must have gone back from whence he came. They were, in fact, two of the coastguards, Messrs Burrell and Kimpton, probably satisfying themselves that there was no funny business going on, Tamzin decided. They were perfectly well ordered and quiet, walking round the outer ring of the castle and smoking their pipes and glancing calmly up at the walls. But the other four, who were two lots of holidaymakers known to each other, kept calling from distant vantage points to those temporarily out of their sight. "Winnee-ee! Can you see them from there?"

"Hallo-oh! Where are you, Fred?" and that kind of thing, continuously and far too loudly for the good of rare and beautiful nesting birds that were, anyhow, strangers in a strange country.

It was all Tamzin could do to restrain herself from rushing at each one of them, saying, "Be *quiet*! Don't you know you're disturbing the hoopoes? Probably the only hoopoes nesting in Britain at this moment – or even at any moment, I expect."

"Oh, if *only* I hadn't put it in the paper!" she suddenly said, nearly in tears of remorse. "I never thought people could be so silly."

"Well, you were really a bit silly, yourself," said Dickon

stolidly, "letting everyone know. Though I don't expect it was only you," he added, seeing her distress, "an' I don't e'spect these people will come again."

"Look! Oh, *look*! There's one of the hoopoes flying!" Tamzin suddenly said, clutching Dickon's shoulder as they stood in the gateway. "Oh, good! Then they've not been frightened away, and they're still all right. Oh, thank goodness for that!"

"I don't think *that's* very 'strornary," said Dickon, staring at the bird in a disillusioned way as it rose and dipped over the wall of the keep. "Not anything like so 'strornary to look at as Jerusalem was." He sighed a small sigh, for a glory that was departed, and stumped after Tamzin over the smooth grass that was like a fitted carpet within the great stone walls.

CHAPTER 16

Developing Danger

The next day, while Tamzin was at school, her mind wandered a great deal because of her anxiety about the hoopoes. It was comforting to reflect how readily the shouting trippers had listened to her parents' (and even her own) explanations about the urgent need for quietness near the nest, the night before, and to think of the notice standing up, propped between two heavy stones, just inside the castle gateway. But all the same, Tamzin was uneasy. She got into trouble three times with three different teachers for not paying attention, but it was no good, her mind was on the hoopoes, and no amount of effort and determination, it seemed, could make it concentrate on learning.

She and Rissa were not in the same form, Rissa being both older and far cleverer, but during the dinner-hour and after school was over they talked about ways of assuring the safety of these strange and beautiful birds.

"Perhaps the excitement will have worn off a bit by now," said Rissa, "and there won't be so many people going out there. Besides, even if there are, your notice is there now to warn them to be careful."

"All the same," said Tamzin, who felt responsible and

almost guilty, "I shall go out again straight after tea, just to make sure. If only it wasn't for school we could have kept a guard there all the time, relieving each other in shifts until the young birds had flown."

"Perhaps I'll come out, too," said Rissa. "I did nearly all my prep. in the dinner hour – did you?"

Tamzin admitted to a total failure in concentration, both over her prep. and at lessons.

"You really are an idiot," said Rissa. "Honestly, the way you let life get you down is almost past believing. Now if you'd been sensible and got on with your homework you'd have had far more time left to help the hoopoes."

"I know." Tamzin looked properly ashamed of herself. "But it seems that's the sort of person I am. I *meant* to do my homework, but it was algebra and geography, and every time I started making myself think of it I found I wasn't."

She was out at the castle that evening long before Rissa, who had to bicycle round by the road, whereas Tamzin could canter fast straight over the grazings and be there in fifteen minutes. Things were not too bad when she got there. Four or five people, strangers to her, were standing watching the hoopoes' flight-line from the willows to the castle, via the flowering may tree, and inside the castle itself she came across the two eldest Lillycrop children, Minerva and Ur, with another Westling boy whom Tamzin only knew as Butterbeans Pope.

Everyone seemed to be observing the care and quietness that the notice appealed for, and no one, so far, had defaced the notice or thrown it away. The sight of various oddments of litter, such as cigarette and chocolate packets, lying about the place, was disturbing, because they indicated the presence of other curious watchers during the day. But to Tamzin's joy the hoopoes were still flying. She stood with Minerva and Ur and Butterbeans for a few minutes, watching the birds thankfully and marvelling at their astonishing trust and tameness. Perhaps they were a little shyer, a little more cautious, pausing nervously in the may tree for just a little longer, raising and lowering their incredible black-tipped crests, before swooping over the walls to their nest in the keep. But perhaps they weren't and it was only Tamzin's imagination.

She went out of the castle again to get Cascade and then rode away down the farm track to meet Rissa. There was no need for either of them to add to the numbers watching the hoopoes, just at present, and it would be good to see the Merrows again, and to deliver Mrs Merrow's *Westling News* in person, for once. But after that she would simply have to ride back hard again and settle down to finish her homework, while Rissa, lucky thing, would most likely be enjoying farmhouse supper with the Merrows.

On Wednesday and Thursday the situation at the castle seemed much the same when Tamzin rode out in the evenings, though each time a few more people were there watching, and a little more litter was on the ground. Meryon and Roger came out on their bicycles on both these evenings, and Rissa and Joseph came once. The worst thing that happened in all this time, as far as anyone could see, was finding the notice broken by stones that had been shied at it, but Meryon and Joseph soon put that right in the Castle Farm workshop, and Joseph found a post to nail it on, so that they could stick it in the ground in a proper and official looking way.

Meryon had really good news about the printing, which helped a lot to balance the general apprehension about the hoopoes.

"I went to see that secretary bloke I told you about as soon as I'd finished tea on Monday, and asked him about printing on the club's machine. He said the club was meeting on the Wednesday and he'd put it to them and let me know today. Rodge and I called in at his house on our way down here, and he said the club didn't see their way to doing any outside printing, but he gave me the address of a retired clerk in Dunsford who does it for a spare-time job, and very reasonably, he says. But that's only if we cut our own stencils and for not less than three dozen copies."

"We've got more than three dozen ordered for next week," said Roger.

"What's a stencil?" Rissa asked, sitting on the work-bench among the spanners and wrenches and paint-pots, dangling her legs.

"A sort of wax sheet, the bloke said. You put them in a typewriter and type just the same as usual, only setting the typewriter properly for stencil-cutting, and the letters come out cut right through, like a painting stencil, only not flowers and things, of course, but letters. Then, when they put that in the duplicator, they can print off as many pages as they like from it, quite quickly."

"Wow!" said Tamzin, marvelling.

"So long as it doesn't come out washy mauve," said Rissa.

"It comes out quite a good black, right to the last copy; he showed me one," said Meryon.

Joseph banged the last nail into the noticeboard and held it up for all to look at. "There, that's as good a notice as ever I saw, and real strong, now. I'll just sharpen the bottom of the post, so's we can bang it into the ground. Pass me that billhook, will you, Roger?"

"We ought to have another notice saying 'Please don't throw stones at this notice'," said Roger, reaching for the billhook.

"What about illustrations?" Rissa asked. "Can we have those with the duplicator? It would be a pity to stop having them."

"He says they're easy, providing you can draw," said Meryon. "You have to get a steel stylus pen, and an old slate off a roof to put under the stencil (really elegant people use a proper writing-plate, but an old slate's just as good, he says), and you just draw. It goes right through, the same as the letters. The whole thing seems to me a fantastic idea, and worth the cost, because we've only got one copy to type out, no matter how many are ordered. And really we are terribly short of time, especially with all this hoopoe-watching in the evenings, as well."

"I don't know about you lot," said Tamzin, "but I've hardly got any news at all for next week. There simply hasn't been time. But perhaps things will get quieter round the hoopoes, soon, and we'll be able to spend more time in the news-hunting and all that."

In fact, the opposite happened, though it was not until the next day that things really began to develop. It all started just after breakfast when Tamzin was getting ready for school, and Smiling Morn brought the vicarage papers across as usual, including, because it was Friday, the *Sussex Herald*. Tamzin glanced up from pumping her bicycle and decided there was just time to have a quick look through it to see if there was anything more about the *Westling News*. There certainly was.

"Oh, Mother, Dad, just look at this!"

"At what?" asked Dickon, pausing in the doorway with his jar of potato leaves which he was just about to take

147

round to the ferry hut before setting off for the village school.

"About our paper——"

"Oh, that," said Dickon, disappointed, and vanished round the doorpost.

"You'll be late for school, dear," said her mother, coming into the kitchen with a trayful of breakfast things.

"No, I won't, I'll go awfully fast. But just look at this!"

The paper was spread out on the kitchen table and Tamzin's hands were spread on the paper as she stared down, reading it. Mrs Grey leaned to read over Tamzin's shoulder, and a moment later Mr Grey was reading over the other one, the coffee-pot that he was carrying still in his hand.

"THE FANTASTIC STRANGERS," they saw in large capitals, the column devoted to news from Westling and district.

"They've used our headline!" Tamzin groaned. "As if it wasn't bad enough mentioning the hoopoes at all."

"They couldn't have known you wanted them kept quiet," her mother reasoned, "after the splash you gave them yourselves."

The vicar read on aloud because Mrs Grey hadn't got her reading glasses in the kitchen.

"'With this arresting headline our enterprising sister-paper, the *Westling News,* begins its second week of publication. And what a scoop this headline announces, a scoop such as many a local, or even daily, paper would print with joy. For these fantastic strangers, so ably hunted out by Westling's efficient young reporters, are no less than a pair of nesting hoopoes. We do not intend to give away any further details, but advise interested readers to get in touch with the editor of the *Westling News,* The Stable-

Loft, Westling Vicarage, who will almost certainly welcome new subscribers and may have spare copies of last week's edition.'"

"Well, that seems very fair to me," said the vicar, taking the coffee-pot out to the scullery. "I wouldn't say they've spiked your guns at all, would you, Gwen? And after all, once the news was spilt it was bound to spread, in a village. More's the pity," he dumped the coffee-pot down and the spoons on the scullery table rattled, "because it would be so much better for the hoopoes if it were otherwise."

Coming back into the kitchen and catching sight of Tamzin's remorseful face he put an arm round her shoulder. "Cheer up, lass! No good crying over spilt news. I dare say it takes any newspaper several years to learn what to put and what not to put in print."

Tamzin bicycled along the Marsh road full of mixed and preoccupying feelings. It was a terrible pity having this further leak-out of news about the hoopoes, just when they were hoping that local curiosity might die down a bit. On the other hand, if it brought them in some new subscribers for the paper it would be a great help towards Jim's fund. But not, oh *not* at the cost of the hoopoes, Tamzin said to herself as she cycled nearer to Dunsford, crowded on its hill beneath its great protecting church.

Coming to the outskirts of the town Tamzin crossed the river bridge at the Strand, looking over at the boats that were moored there for unloading timber and coal, and then suddenly, out of the corner of her eye, she saw the word "hoopoes". It is very strange how the eye will pick out a word that matters, when you aren't looking for it or expecting it at all, sometimes from the middle of a sheet of newspaper or, as with Tamzin now, from a distant notice that in the ordinary way she would never have seen at all.

149

The effect on her was instantaneous. Glancing urgently across the Strand again to make quite sure, she would have run into a man wheeling coke in a barrow from the gasworks to a boat, if he had not shouted; and then, trying to avoid him, she set up a wobble that nearly had her off her bicycle for the second time that week.

"You better be careful, you had," the man shouted, stopping to pick up some fragments of coke that had rolled off his barrow in the general struggle for evasion.

"I'm awfully sorry!" Tamzin called back apologetically over her shoulder and nearly ran into an old man mending nets between the river and the road. After this she dismounted to say how sorry she was again, and then walked across the road to read the notice. It was printed rather clumsily in red chalk letters on a large blackboard which was propped against the wall, and it said:

"First Conducted Outing to the Castle Hoopoes. Starting 2.30 p.m. tomorrow, Saturday. Book now: Galley, Ship Inn, Strand."

Tamzin stared at it like a blind person seeing for the first time. She stared at it blankly and for so long that already she would have been late for school. And then she suddenly turned and jumped on her bicycle and pedalled fast down the road towards "The Ship".

CHAPTER 17

Anything's Always Worth Trying

It was not the hour of opening for inns, a thing that Tamzin often got mixed up about because of their times being different from those of shops. "The Ship Inn" was officially shut, but the door was open and a woman was swabbing out the tiled floor with a mop and bucket. In response to Tamzin's anxious inquiry she said that she did not expect Mr Galley or, indeed, anyone else at all, until turned half-past ten, which was the proper time, and Tamzin shouldn't be in a pub anyway. Tamzin took a step backwards over the threshold, and in doing so somehow trod on the tail of a black-and-brown dog that had suddenly appeared there, so that it nipped her ankle and made her jump badly. What with this, and the thought that she had hurt the dog, and would miss Hookey Galley, and had twice nearly fallen off her bicycle in the last fifteen minutes, and would now certainly be very late for school, Tamzin went back to her propped-up machine in a state of profound despair. But bigger than all these trials and vexations was the stark thought, standing up in her mind like a doom, of the First Conducted Outing to the hoopoes.

Imagining even one bus load of curious trippers crowding into the hoopoes' solitude, Tamzin tried to speculate on the effect of a whole series, and found she simply couldn't. Pedalling desolately back along the Strand and round into the Cinque Ports Street she was so troubled by this new threat to the hoopoes that she hardly even thought about the consequences of arriving nearly half an hour late for school.

Her reputation for lack of concentration (never very high, but shockingly low in the last few days) dropped on this day to previously unplumbed levels, and if anyone had asked her, as she and Rissa pedalled out of the school gates that evening, to tell them one thing that she had learned during the day, she could not have done so. They went, together, straight to the Strand where Tamzin showed Rissa, speechlessly, the deadful notice, and then they went on in troubled silence to the old "Ship Inn".

"Mind that dog; it sits with its tail across the doorway," Tamzin said abstractedly, and then remembered that they were not allowed inside. Peering into the cool interior shadows that smelt of beer and geraniums, they saw the man they wanted, propped on his navy-guernseyed elbow at the bar and talking to half a dozen strangers.

"Oh, it's you again," said the woman who had been swabbing the floor and was serving behind the bar. "If you're looking for Mr Galley, he's here."

Tamzin saw money and blue tickets changing hands, and then Hookey turned round to face them, smiling widely at the thought of more business, when business was being so fast and good in any case.

"Only three seats left," he was saying complacently, and then recognised the faces in the doorway.

"Your first customer today, that little one was," said the

barmaid. "Here just on nine o'clock, asking for you, weren't you, ducks? Well, it looks as if they're just in time for this trip, eh, Hookey? Though there's always more trips later on."

Hookey knew that, whatever Tamzin and Rissa wanted him for, it was not for places on his outing. Moreover, knowing them well, he didn't want any funny business in front of his customers, such as might cause them to ask for their money back, so that he strode to the doorway in his lean, jerky way, boring his hawkish glance into their faces, and said they could speak to him outside. He led them clear of the inn and the interested hovering customers who still had their tickets in their hands, to the edge of the wharf where "Jacob's ladders" went down abruptly to the moored boats and barges, and seagulls glided and planed with desolate cries that made Tamzin's heart feel sadder and heavier. Hookey sat down on a bollard and glanced up sideways, and all he said was, "Well?"

Tamzin looked at him despairingly, knowing that nothing either of them said would have any effect, but being determined to say it.

"Hookey, it's the hoopoes . . ." She looked at Rissa now, in the sudden wild hope that she might rush in with a flow of well-chosen words that would leave Hookey absolutely vanquished and convinced, but Rissa said nothing at all, feeling that as far as anyone could possibly know Hookey, Tamzin knew him better than she did.

"Well?" said Hookey again, deliberately beginning to roll a cigarette.

"You can't – you *mustn't* take people out to see them!" Tamzin cried, scrabbling in her mind for words to express what she was feeling. "They're so rare and beautiful, we've got to give them a chance – don't you *see* – they'll be

153

frightened by crowds of people, and probably desert their nest and young – oh, you must see *that*?"

Hookey put a match calmly to his cigarette and lit it.

"They're only birds," he said. "They don't matter like we do. You eat chickens, don't you? Well, ent they got as much right to peace as what hoopoes have? Tell me the difference."

Already Tamzin was baffled. What *was* the difference? Were rarity and beauty alone such sacred things? But, if not, why was it all right to slash a nettle and not a magnolia? To eat a hen but not a nightingale? If Hookey couldn't see it, no words of hers could make any difference, but she blundered on.

"But they've come to make their nest in Britain – perhaps the only ones that ever have – and they've made it in our castle, trusting us. Oh, can't you *see*, Hookey? It's historic, it's a trust. We've got to protect them. Even if they were ordinary birds it would be only right, now they're rearing young. People don't eat hens that are rearing chicks, or do anything that might mean the chicks being deserted and left to die."

"To my mind," said Hookey in a voice as calm as hers was excited, "You're just plain silly – silly and un-businesslike. Look at the money as is to be made out of these birds – what are only birds, when all's said and done. Farmers make money out of hens and pigs and such, don't they? Well, I'm making money out of hoopoes. Easy money," he grinned at her, jingling coins in his pocket. "So could you, if you got any business sense. Conducted ramblings from Westling, see. Photos of the nest. That sort of thing."

Rissa snorted disgustedly, like a horse offered dog-meat, but Tamzin just stared in disbelieving horror.

154

"I got as much right to a living as the next man," said Hookey, becoming aggressive now. "What I say is, it's every man for himself in this ruddy world. No one else won't help you, except yourself, and if you don't grab what's there for grabbing, someone else will. The bloke what gets on is the bloke what gets there first. That's me, this time. Hired a nice liddle bus, I have, from a private comp'ny; wrote out me notice and sold all me tickets already, except for three. And I lay there's folks waiting for them at the 'Ship', this minute, so if you'll excuse me——" he stood up with exaggerated politeness, "I'll be getten along."

Tamzin looked at him in awestruck sadness.

"What an awful thing to think of life like that. If it were me, I'd rather be dead."

"Well, of course," said Hookey, "you're a parson's daughter, and I suppose you got to think according. But let me tell you, it's only money what talks in this world. And arter that we're dead, ent we? So why not get everything out of life while you can? If we don't, someone else will." He strolled away, hands in pockets, coins jingling, and Tamzin stood there with Rissa, hearing in the mists of her mind her father saying, "Life isn't a cup to drain, but a cup to fill."

Hookey paused at the edge of the road and looked over his shoulder. "Perhaps they wunt fly away," he said, in a kind of off-hand effort at self-justification. "We're only going to *look* at them, arter all. And the sooner we frit 'em away, the sooner the money stops – stands to reason." Then he turned and vanished through the doorway of "The Ship".

"I knew it wouldn't be any good talking to him," said Rissa, kicking at the dust and pebbles of the Strand.

Tamzin began walking slowly back to the bicycles, propped against the wall of the inn. "Anything's always worth trying," she said in a tired kind of voice, "even if you do know it won't be any good."

"Well, what are we going to do now?"

Tamzin shook her head. "See what Meryon and Roger think, perhaps – and Mother and Dad – everyone that we can get on our side. I don't think I mind what we have to do to save the hoopoes, if only we can do it somehow because it was all my fault that they were put in so much danger."

"What nonsense," said Rissa bracingly, grasping her handlebars and whisking her bicycle round to face the road. "You and Roger both found them. And you weren't the first, even then, because Johnny Beatup was. He would probably have spread it round almost as fast as the *Westling News* did, even if you hadn't written about them at all."

"But he didn't, and I did," said Tamzin sadly. "It really was *me,* you know. Roger wasn't very keen on going out to the castle, then. He only came because I said so."

"And now," said Rissa with her foot on the pedal, "I suppose you'll feel you've got to sacrifice yourself in a kind of atonement, or something."

Tamzin shook her head. "There isn't really very much to atone for, yet. What I want to do is stop something happening that we would all feel awful about. We oughtn't to have put about the hoopoes in the paper. We can all see that now, but we didn't any of us realise what a lot of people would actually go out to look at them. I knew people would be very interested, of course, the way everyone is in any unusual news, but I somehow never thought so many would want to *go* there, or that the news would spread so far. I know it seems silly, but that's the way it is, and I think it's true of all of us, too, or obviously we wouldn't have put it in."

"I'll tell you what occurs to me," said Rissa as they cycled along the Strand and over the bridge, "we're going to have an awful sweat getting the paper off, this weekend. We've got to do it, of course, or customers will just drop us wholesale; but how many of us are going to be free for news-gathering and writing-up and typing, with a busload of sightseers scheduled to visit the hoopoes tomorrow afternoon? And probably another on Sunday."

"I don't know," Tamzin said, "but I expect we'll do it, because we've *got* to do it. The others may have some ideas, and there's always Joseph, and with you coming to tea today we've got the whole of this evening. Thank goodness, anyway, for Meryon's duplicator man. We'll only have one copy to type, always providing Meryon's been able to get the stencils and the stylus and everything. And I've got an old slate that fell off the stable roof. I expect it'll have to be put back on again before the winter, but at least we can use it till then."

"I was just thinking," said Rissa, "that when the young hoopoes have flown, and we've paid Jim's debt at Mr Henzie's, and school has broken up, we'll simply have oceans and oceans of time on our hands – lovely, long, endless time! We'll be so out practice we shan't know what to do with it."

"Of course we shall," said Tamzin, turning left into the Westling road. "Anyway, I've never found that any day was half long enough for all I wanted to do in it."

CHAPTER 18

Plea for the Hoopoes

Cycling into the village, past the church and school, Tamzin and Rissa saw a swirl of pebbly dust fly up, away down the road at Smiling Morn's corner, and two dogs and a small boy leapt for the roadside.

"That's Jim, I expect," said Tamzin, and it was.

"It's astonishing to me," said Rissa, "that he hasn't killed or crippled either himself or anyone else, yet, the pace he goes."

But while she was still speaking Smiling Morn stepped out from his shop with a great box loaded full of groceries that impeded his already short vision. It was difficult to be sure just what did happen then, but Tamzin was convinced that the grocer and the wheelchair actually made a complete circle round each other, like partners in a country dance, before Jim shot away again and came roaring up the village, leaving Smiling Morn standing dazed in the middle of the street surrounded by groceries. Outside the post office the wheelchair came to a sudden stop and the ferryman leaped nimbly out, leaving his crutches sticking up beside the driving seat, and ran across the road to post a letter. Tamzin and Rissa came pedalling up as he turned round to dash back to his chair, and at once the old man started limping.

"Isn't your leg much better, Jim?" Tamzin asked innocently. "We thought you ran across to the letterbox really well, and I was just saying to Rissa that you'd soon have finished with the chair."

The ferryman glared at her suspiciously. "I wuz just posting a letter from my Dad to ole Aunt Ada, see, and I been and disremembered me leg were bad, thass all," he said, leaning heavily on the side of his carriage. "Soon as I realised it were hurting smartish I eased off 'un a bit, a'course." He climbed painfully into the wheelchair as one whose every movement agonised him, and then sitting down in it, smiled suddenly up at Tamzin. "Ah! thass better. Dunno where I'd be without me ole goo-chair, that I don't. You – er——you wunt goo telling Vicar as I nipped across without me crutches, gal, now will you? They just slipped me mind, like, you unnerstand. Gor bless us, I wouldn't want the vicar to go thinking as I done finished wid me chair."

"All right, Jim," said Tamzin, grinning in spite of herself.

"But I wish I could run at that speed, all the same," said Rissa, "and I daresay Mr Goldeye did, too. He's picking up his groceries now. Perhaps we ought to help him, Tamzin."

"I seem always to be helping him pick up something," said Tamzin, remembering the peas, which had in a way been the start of all the trouble with the hoopoes.

Old Jim pulled at his starter. "Dang me if I wunt give ole Corpse-Face a hand, meself," he said, flipping off his hand-brake, "so long as no one don't hold it again me doing it without me crutches. You carsn't pick up groceries whiles you're hampered wid a pair of crutches, now can you, gal? Stands to reason."

Automatically, Tamzin began to frame a newspaper column in her mind as the three of them helped the grocer to gather up yet more split peas, as well as six pounds of chicken corn that had exuberantly spread about the road:

"UNFORTUNATE ACCIDENT TO NOTED WESTLING GROCER.

While carrying a loaded box of groceries across the road from his shop, Mr E. Goldeye miraculously avoided a collision with our famous ferryman in his motor wheelchair. There were no casualties, except for a pound and a half of split peas and six pounds of corn, which were ably picked up by willing helpers. Other groceries, remaining in their packets and tins and boxes, presented few difficulties in retrieving."

"About time Some People took their driving test," said Mr Goldeye, grumbling obliquely but never looking at Jim Decks. "If they could, that is, which they probably couldn't. Some never can, and if you ask me the party in question is one." He sighed heavily, taking his weight on the other leg because bending was not very convenient to his middle-aged spread. "I was thinking, Tamzin," he went on sadly, "that Mrs Goldeye and myself might place an order for your little paper, perhaps. We didn't see it at all this week, as you delivered it personally." Tamzin's face showed nothing, but a triumphant grin spread over her mind. "But the price, of course, is quite exhorbitant." He sighed again, dropping hen-corn into the large brown paper bag that stood open in the roadway.

"We hope to lower the price eventually," Rissa said encouragingly, "if the circulation goes up enough," but the ferryman glowered sideways across the grocery box, remarking that Some People would grudge a penny to pay for their own coffin, and if one person could talk at the air in general, so could two.

In the vicarage kitchen, a few minutes later, Tamzin and Rissa were astonished to learn that all kinds of people had been telephoning, off and on, all day.

"One or two were our own friends in and around Dunsford," said Tamzin's mother. "Two very nice people offered to do shifts at guarding the hoopoes, and there were two new orders for the *Westling News* – I wrote the names and addresses down in the telephone book – though none for back numbers: but we had inquiries about the birds from total strangers, too – people who'd read about them in the *Herald*." Tamzin gazed at her in consternation, but Mrs Grey tranquilly continued cutting brown bread and butter. "Of course, I said to everyone that we were very anxious not to have the hoopoes disturbed, and I think every single person Richard and I spoke to understood that. But Mrs Gasson told me about Hookey's conducted outings." She opened another packet of butter. "I was very sorry about that. What an awkward man he always is. And I suppose nothing we might do or say would make any difference."

"Nothing that Tamzin said made any difference," Rissa told her. "We saw him in Dunsford and she tried hard to make him see how important it was to leave them in peace, but he wouldn't."

"The first busload goes out tomorrow afternoon," said Tamzin, "and we're going to be there – some of us, anyway. I wish we knew how old the young ones are, and when they would be old enough to fly."

"Has Dicky found his Colorado yet?" Rissa asked,

beginning to count plates and saucers on to the trolley for Mrs Grey.

"Not yet, but he doesn't lose hope. He's been writing an article for your paper, as he says he hasn't found much news for it owing to searching for Jerusalem all the time. It's just there, on the dresser, by the knife-box."

Tamzin picked it up, all ready typed, quite neatly, on his father's typewriter. It was called "The Howbl Deth", and it went like this:

"The wind blo it must be a gayl. It's freesing, Look overe theyer, it,s snoing it was just rite for them, And thay got the sleg owt and the storm was geting werser and nerer, and sudnly a grayte drift caym down and cuverd evry child rite overe, and thay have only just been fownd, and only wun was left with scin on, all the rest wer sckelitns. Presntly the hole vilig was berid,

> And all the uther viligs cride like this ,,,,,,,,,,,,
> And the sno fel like this ....
> And the rane fel like this ///////////////
> And it was a howbl deth."

She passed it to Rissa, grinning appreciatively. "I don't know about it's coming quite up to our standard and it's almost X Certificate, but I dare say we'll be glad to have it, the way things are!"

Early in the evening Meryon and Roger arrived, to Tamzin's relief, as they couldn't always get away in term-time evenings, and they had brought both a packet of stencils and the steel stylus. Tamzin would have liked to try the stencil at once on the typewriter, but her father was using the machine and, in any case, the evening was going to be short as it was for all the news-gathering that had to be done.

"Of course, the paper'll come out a day later now – we can't avoid that," Meryon was saying as they inspected his purchases in the stable loft office. "You'll have to take the stencil in on Monday mornings, Tamzin – the bloke lives in Cinque Ports Street, right on your route – and then call for the finished papers on your way home. They could be at the post office the same evening, I suppose, for anyone to collect who likes their news hot."

"What d'you think about this Hookey Galley outing business?" Rissa asked. "Tamzin and I found him pretty stubborn about it, when we saw him in the morning."

"Of course, he's cashing-in on the *Herald* write-up," said Roger. "Everyone knows about the hoopoes, now."

"He'd sold nearly all his tickets before half-past four," said Tamzin, beginning to wrinkle up with worry again.

"Well, short of puncturing all the tyres on both of Dunsford's small private buses, I don't see how we can stop the party going out there," said Meryon, "but some of us ought to be at the castle when they're there, just in case we can keep them fairly quiet and reasonably far away. Of course, they might quite easily take no notice of us, at all, as we're so young and they'll have Hookey with them, but we can at least try."

"Hey, I've got an idea!" said Tamzin with sudden inspiration. "What about old Jim's telescope? It's a really good one, and I'm sure he'd lend it if we explained how much it would help. We could offer everyone who doesn't go *inside* the castle a free look at the hoopoes through it."

"It *is* quite a good idea," said Roger enthusiastically. "I'd like a look at them through it, myself."

"It's your turn to do that side of the village this

evening," Rissa said to Tamzin, "so you can ask him about it. I suppose Roger teams up with you, this time?"

"But if we change partners as well as districts every time," Meryon said, "two of us don't get a change of district."

"All right, let's just change districts," said Rissa obligingly, though feeling annoyed about it because more exciting things always seemed to happen to Meryon than to Roger, though with Roger one did have the reflected glory of news-hunting with the editor himself. "Is anyone going out to look at the hoopoes?"

"One of the people who phoned offering to help – he's a school teacher, Dad said – is going out," said Tamzin, "so I don't think any of us need, until tomorrow. That gives us the whole evening on the paper."

"What news have we got already, to start with?" asked Roger, who found it difficult not living nearer to the centre of his work. He opened his notebook. "I've done a thing about the Royal Lifeboat Institution, that I swotted up from a book of Dad's, and Meryon's got the competition worked out, though we haven't got a prize yet."

"We didn't have any entries at all for last week's," said Tamzin. "Everyone I asked said it couldn't be done, just the same as I said myself, so at least we've still got Dad's green notepaper for this week's prize. What's the competition?"

"For the best map of Westling," Meryon said. "I wouldn't mind having a bash at it myself, as I rather like drawing maps, but I suppose the editor and staff are banned from their own competitions."

"People can put in the shoreline, with ships and dolphins and things, if they like," said Roger, "and Shirty Smeed's bloater-smoking shed, and Jim's ferryboat, and the Deeproses' cows.''

"And all the Lillycrop children filing in at their gate!" grinned Rissa.

"And Banner and Cascade in their paddock," said Tamzin, "and the Harbour Mast, and the little lighthouse, and the Martello tower."

"Any real news?" asked Roger.

Tamzin showed him Dickon's story and her own rough draught of the Unfortunate Accident to Noted Westling Grocer. "I had thought of putting in a bulletin about Jim – how he's getting on so well – but he seems touchy about people thinking he might do without his wheelchair."

"If no one collects his old *Emma* pretty soon," said Rissa, "she may have to go to grass or something, because Dad wants the shed-room for a lathe he's putting up in there."

"I don't think there's any more *news*, yet," Tamzin said, "but we ought to put in a plea for the hoopoes, I think. You know, something about the awful risk to them of people crowding round, and asking as many as possible to stay away, or at least not to go too near. I did start a thing in the evenings during the week. It's called, 'Plea For Our Hoopoes', and so far I've said, 'Westling's hoopoes – probably Britain's only hoopoes – are in danger. These rare birds may desert their nest and young if crowds continue to increase around them. Please help to protect our hoopoes! You can do this by keeping away from Cloudesley Castle until the young have flown, and by asking other people to do so, too'. That's as far as I've got."

"It seems very complete and good to me," said Rissa critically.

"Perhaps you could add, say, 'In this way you might find that you have helped, not only to protect Westling's

165

hoopoes, but to establish this beautiful breed as a recognised British bird'," suggested Meryon.

"Yes, that's quite good," said Tamzin, and wrote it down, kneeling up to the goat-bench.

"We must try to get some more advertisements," Roger said. "We haven't got any this week, and they do pay."

"Fred Downing will put another in," said Tamzin. "Meryon and I can see him about that, this evening. And you and Rissa could try for a chickens, egg and dairy cream one from Harbour Farm. Smiling Morn is really rather a hopeless quest, and I can't think of anyone else at the moment."

While they were pondering on this, just before setting out into the village, they heard light steps on the stable ladder and all looked expectantly at the hole where it emerged into the loft. The visitor was Gypsophila Lilly-crop, who was only seven but quite sensible, perhaps because of living in such a very enormous family. She wore a faded blue dress that was too big for her, and her long, lank blonde hair hung unbrushed around her thin shoulders.

"I come from Mus Galley," she said shyly, pausing near the top of the ladder and looking along the floor to where a collection of legs in jeans and bare brown skin were just at her eye-level, round the goat-bench.

"What, Hookey?" said Roger, very surprised. "Good lord! Well, come along up."

Gypsophila climbed from the ladder to the floor and approached uncertainly, a piece of crumpled paper in her hand.

"What on earth does Hookey want, Gypsophila?" Tamzin asked, hope rising and pushing down a fearful doubt. "Come and sit on the desk. We haven't many seats

166

in the office yet, I'm afraid – only the soap-box for the editor."

"And he'd really be more comfortable on the floor," said Rissa, "only that wouldn't be in keeping with his editorial position."

"Here you are," said Gypsophila, thrusting the paper at them all in general. "Mus Galley says give it to 'em, he says, and this as well."

She unclutched her hand from a hot, sticky coin which the editor placed carefully on the goat-bench while he studied the piece of paper.

"Hey, I say! It's an advertisement – about his conducted outings," he exclaimed, scarcely believing it. "Honestly – just look. Can you imagine him thinking we'd put that in?"

"He jus' said give you it," said Gypsophila, "and he give me twopence to come. Can I go now?" She was half turned, her weight on one dusty brown leg.

"Oh, just a minute!" Tamzin said to her, glancing up for a second from the paper. "I think you'll just have to take it back to him, Gyp. He must have *known* we wouldn't put it in. Look at it, Riss: it's practically the same as the Strand notice, only giving his Westling address as well."

"The absolute *nerve* of it!" snorted Rissa.

"He said tell you you was to put it in," said Gypsophila. "If I take it back, he'll take my twopence what he gave me, won't he?"

"Well, he flipping well oughtn't to," exclaimed Roger righteously. "He gave it to you for bringing the paper, not for our accepting it."

Meryon looked up and saw the child's sad and disillusioned face, thin and framed by her lank fair hair, and was suddenly filled with compassion. "Well, look, supposing we give you twopence to take it back to him. If he takes his twopence away you've still got one, and if he doesn't you've got two!"

Gypsophila's sad face softened into a shining smile, and she took Meryon's coin, and Hookey's offering and padded across the floorboards to the ladder again. At the top, balanced backwards half over the edge of the square ladder-hole, she turned and smiled again. "I say, thanks ever so! Thanks really ever so!" And her blonde head went down in little jerks until it was out of sight below the floor.

"Well, I suppose that's as good a way of spending twopence as any!" said Meryon philosophically.

Rissa swung round and glared at him incredulously, her heavy brown bobbed hair swishing across her eyes so that she had the look of a furious Skye terrier. "I just don't know how you can joke like that, so calmly, when Hookey's done such a bare-faced and astonishing thing."

"Oh, I don't know that it's so astonishing, when you come to think of it – and of Hookey," Meryon said. "It's rather in character, really. I expect he thinks we're all really ignorant, and that we probably think a paper *has* to print an advertisement for anyone, whether it likes it or not."

"Even I know that isn't true," said Tamzin. "I remember seeing in a paper of Dad's that they 'accept advertisements at their own discretion'."

"But Hookey doesn't know you know that. He probably doesn't even know it, himself. And can't you just imagine his pleasure in thinking that he's *made* us support his conducted outings, in spite of ourselves! At least, from my knowledge of Hookey I think that's the kind of thing he would enjoy."

Tamzin sighed. "I just don't know why anyone wants to be so full of hate and perversity. Anyone would think——"

Meryon gave her hair a warning tug. "Now, Tamzin, we'd better get hot on the trail of some news, or if there isn't any, make some, or the *Westling News* will never come out this week at all."

CHAPTER 19

In Spite of Every Threat

Working from Dunsford View downwards, and taking in the post office and Coastguard Houses and Smiling Morn's shop, Tamzin and Meryon set out to cover their half of the village methodically. At the Dunsford View cottages they were again rebuffed and shouted at by Mrs Venus, who was hanging washing on a line in her back yard.

"It's Mrs One-Who-Knows," said Tamzin as they walked along the fences. "She doesn't really matter – she's like that with everyone. Let's try Mrs Shaggy Apps. She's rather nice; anyone must be, to live next door to Mrs Venus and still have so few enemies."

Mrs Apps was indeed delighted to see them both, and told them a long tale about how her husband, Shaggy, had got caught in the quicksands when he was longshore fishing a day or two before, being rescued by Truggy Upjohn when he was already up to his knees. And then she placed an order for the paper and said that her sister in Hastings would have one, too. This was a good beginning which was fortified by Fred Downing at the post office putting in the new advertisement about Instant Summer Puddings, and suggesting an Exchange, Sale and Wanted column, which Tamzin and Meryon thought might be quite a good idea, with a charge of about tenpence for each small entry.

"I could start it off with one of my own," said Tamzin. "'Exchange: two slightly shabby dressed dolls (outgrown) for haynet. Adapted fish-net considered.' Cascade always chews his, and they're so expensive to buy."

The coastguards were all very reserved and secretive, as usual, probably thinking that any news they did have was bound to be connected with illicit free trade activities, even if it was only Mr Kimpton's having had all his teeth out.

Smiling Morn was sitting on a box of apples behind his counter, in a swoon of deep melancholy because of the non-arrival of a crate of Dazzo Washing Powder which was very popular throughout the whole village, so he was not much use. Cheerful little Mrs Goldeye came whisking into the shop like a small rubber barrel and danced a hornpipe on the counter for them – a thing she was famed for in more than five towns and villages – but that wasn't really much use, either, because it wasn't news.

Round at the Point the first person they encountered was Dickon, squatting on the shingle beside an upturned boulder-boat and watching intently a sprig of sad-looking potato leaves that he had planted in its shade. This wasn't really news, either, and the whole evening's activities were beginning to seem rather depressing, until Tamzin caught sight of two very old, white haired men leaning busily over a stripped-down wheelchair.

"Jim! Oh, hallo!" she called. "Good morning, Mr Decks," she added politely to the older man, whom she had not met more than once or twice before owing to extreme pressure of time.

The two white heads emerged from the secret places of the wheelchair and grinned at her encouragingly. This looked hopeful. Old Jim (or *could* you say "old Jim," now

171

that he had suddenly produced an older one?) was in a good mood. The prospects for the telescope brightened at once in her anxious mind as she strode forward over the still-warm shingle.

"Something wrong with the limousine?" Meryon asked with interest as they approached, and Tamzin was silent with the fascination of seeing these two extraordinary men together; so alike but so unlike: both of them rugged, immensely tough and bold looking, but whereas the ferryman was cantankerous and mercurial in his moods (and therefore in his expressions) his father surveyed the world from a private fortress of enormous calm and serenity.

"We was having a bit of a tinker wid her back axle, on account of she ent got no differential," said the ferryman. "You call to mind how she nips round righthand corners mighty fast, I dessay? Well, she goo round left 'uns just as tedious slow."

"Oh yes, of course she would," said Meryon, understanding immediately, although to Tamzin nothing could have been more obscure. He turned to her. "The engine only actually drives one wheel," he said explanatorily, "the right one. That would make her twice as fast round Smiling Morn's corner, going out, as it would coming back."

"Oh, I see," said Tamzin doubtfully, suddenly grinning as she remembered her own and Smiling Morn's disasters near that corner. "What are you going to do, Jim? Make the right wheel slower or the left one faster?"

But the old man only grunted. "Hey, Dad, chuck me the spanner," he said. "I gotta tidy gret nut here what's too big by half for this tiddly liddle 'un."

The patriarch tossed it capably and then wiped his hands down his sailcloth trousers and smiled at Tamzin, so there wasn't much to be seen of his face except a brown multitude of smile-wrinkles in a meringue of foaming white hair and beard. Baldness did not run in the Decks family, and young Jimmy was probably the first male in their history to have no beard.

Tamzin smiled back, and presently it was Meryon's head in the depths of the wheelchair with old Jim's while Tamzin and the patriarch sat on the ferry hut bench and talked about differentials, speed limits, buses, hoopoes and telescopes.

"That telescope," said older Jim, "is by way of being a family one, Miss. My ole dad he give it to me, and – come the time he were old enough to look arter it proper – I give it young Jim there."

Young Jim! Tamzin thought, amused by the idea of anyone's being both old Jim and young Jim at one and the same time.

"Do you think he would lend it to us, Mr Decks? If we could have it just for tomorrow – but much better for all the days until the hoopoes fly – it would be a simply tremendous help."

"Well now, gal——" Mr Decks was looking away down the river at the boats and the scintillating water and the seagulls making their cats'-cradles in the milky blueness over it – "Well, gal, it ent so much would *Jim* lend it as would I. You look at it thisaway, ole young 'un; he's a good boy, is young Jim, but he's still ower wild and thoughtless. 'Course he'll mebbe grow outen it, in time, and steady down like, but we gotta have patience. He don' properly appreciate the value of that telescope yet, as he will, time he gits older. Well now, gal, can you borrer it, you arst? I say you can borrer it under proper supervision."

Tamzin's hopes rose. "Meryon would be with us. That's Meryon, there. He's really sensible and careful and much older than I am."

Older Jim turned and subjected Meryon to a searching scrutiny, which produced the judgment that he was "ower young, gal; ower by half. No, it gotta be young Jim hisself or better still, me, as sits beside you."

Tamzin looked at him dubiously. "I don't think it would be the best road for Jim in the wheelchair; and I don't know how you would get there at all, because it's quite a long walk, over sheep-tracks and all that."

Mr Decks returned her look with immense dignity and reproof. "I knowed that hem ole castle afore your granfer were thought of," he said. "The distance is lessen a half-hour's stroll, as the sheep walks. Now let me tell you, ole young 'un, I wager I could walk you orf your own two legs any day you like to name. So what?"

The idea was quite incredible, but Tamzin's face spread into a slow broad smile. "Would you really come, and bring the telescope? Tomorrow afternoon? We'd call for you, of course, Mr Decks."

"We-ell now, I *could*, of course, as I just done said," said Mr Decks, sounding for a moment almost like old Jim when Jim was hedging, "but whether I'll be able for to fit it in, I do hardly know. Young Jim, there, is that dead keen to goo racing about in his ole wheelchair while he got it, see, and that only leave me to run the ruddy ferry."

"Oh, but he won't want to be out in the wheelchair *all* the time, surely." Tamzin exclaimed. "You could come just for the afternoon?" Fantastic visions crossed her mind of Meryon and Roger sabotaging the wheelchair by dropping soap in the petrol tank, or grit in the plugs, or whatever it was that you did to immobilise a motor engine. But, suddenly and wonderfully, it seemed as if these extreme measures would not be necessary. The patriarch slapped his hard tough hands down on his knees and directed a piercing blue look at her.

"Right, gal, I will! Blow me if I wunt. Young Jim can do as his dad say, for once, and do him good too. I allus did say as you gotta be firm wid young 'uns 'r else they never will grow up right, stands to reason. An another thing; I ent never seen a hoopoe, though I done travelled all the world over in me time, and seen kiwis and ostriches and hummingbirds and dunnamany gret wild animals. Real fond of birds, I wuz." He sighed reminiscently, lapsing into thought, and Tamzin sat radiantly by his side in the evening sunshine, clasping the ferry cat and thinking of tomorrow and the telescope and how everyone was fighting for the hoopoes, and perhaps all would work out for their safety after all, in spite of every threat and danger. . . . Someone pulled her hair and she glanced up.

"Come on, young 'un," said Meryon, looking rather more wild-haired than usual owing to the inside of the wheelchair, "we've got to push on up the river in a last minute rake-up of news. Jim says there's a Dutch trader up there with a monkey that they've trained as a deck-hand, as well as a yacht with a Russian Grand Duke on board. They don't have any aristocracy over there since the Revolution, of course, because of everybody being equal; Jim says he wears oily jeans and looks like a third mate, but all the same, he is a Russian nobleman."

"It'll make some news, anyway," said Tamzin, "and we don't seem to have very much in that line, after all last week's excitements. Shall we walk up or row up?"

"Take young Jimmy's *Kittiwake*," said Jim, "'r else you won't be able to reach the Russian, without you swim, fer the reason as he's tied up on the Dunsmere side, gal. Tide's making, so pull her up smartish when you git back, see."

175

It was pure pleasure rowing upstream on the flowing tide, which always made the river look as if it were running the wrong way. No effort was required from Meryon at the oars except to keep the dinghy headed straight, and he and Tamzin looked at all the boats as they glided between them, and at the sunset colours on the water that made a crimson river under a small black boat.

Tamzin and Meryon found that there was only one trouble with the crew of the Dutchman, when they had tied up against her, and that was that none of them spoke English at all, though they were very friendly and anxious to be of use. Their coasting trader was a beautifully kept boat, nearly all hold and enormous hatches but swept and polished, and with flowers in pots hanging in the skylights and secured to the bulkheads, and even curtains at the chart-room and wheelhouse windows. They saw the monkey, and Tamzin even saw it coiling down a rope, but by the time she had diverted Meryon from his interest in the mixed cargo of Dutch white bricks and fertiliser the monkey had tired of doing this and was pursuing fleas along its arm again.

The Grand Duke, on the other hand, had quite a smattering of English and was simply longing to try it out. He was a most hospitable though shockingly untidy man, and would certainly have kept Tamzin and Meryon on board his dilapidated yacht until far past midnight had they been willing and able. As things were, there was only about half an hour before they were due back at the office, but a great deal of cheerful and incredible English conversation was packed into this brief time, which ended with the Grand Duke bowing them out of his cabin and saying courteously, "Ah, my children, how can I regret you? Your visit has enjoyed me very much, for I am refuged of my own country, and every time a stranger."

As Meryon rowed the *Kittiwake* back down the river to the Hard, the masts of moored boats were already black against the fire of the evening sky, and the tide, though still making, had stretched the river so wide that it was like a burning lake. They pulled the dinghy up well above the high-water mark, tied her to the mooring-post and trudged back over the shingle to the stable loft office, where there was barely time left to make the roughest assembly of material for the next number of the *Westling News*.

"Tomorrow," said Meryon, thrusting his hands through his jungle hair, "we must work in shifts. Either Rodge or I will stay at the castle all the morning – we shan't be able to see the grass for people, I expect, on a Saturday morning – and perhaps Joseph will be able to come, too. Whichever of us isn't at the castle will come here and help with the write-up, and we'll swap over in the afternoon."

"It really will be terrific if we can get the telescope," said Roger, "but does anyone think that that prehistoric old man will be able to *walk* there?"

Tamzin grinned. "I think so, enough not to've taken on his bet that he could walk me off my legs!"

"His generation are like oak timbers," Meryon said. "The older they are the harder they get."

"I know," said Rissa. "There's a house in our street with beams so hard they can't knock nails into them."

"What happens when they try?" Roger asked with interest.

"The nails bend," said Rissa, suddenly yawning. "Hey! Look at the time. Is anyone for the road?"

CHAPTER 20

A Man in Authority

Tamzin felt very distracted on the Saturday morning. The day began with a really large-scale shock in the shape of a detailed paragraph about the hoopoes in Mr Briggs's daily paper, which she rushed round for the vicarage family to look at. And on Tamzin's hasty and anxious dash up to the post office to ask Fred Downing if she might glance through some of the other papers, she found that the news was in almost every one. This alone was unsettling enough, but there were several more telephone calls from curious strangers before breakfast was over, and then Meryon arrived, troubled and alone, while she was dusting the downstairs rooms, which was her house job for that day.

"Give me another duster," he said, "and I can help while I natter."

Tamzin found him the remains of one of her father's old shirts and he began whisking it efficiently round the chairs and tables, not forgetting the legs and staves as so many did. "Rodge and I picked up Joseph quite early and set out for the castle, and though you'd hardly believe it, there were people there already. We could see several more in the distance, coming along the sheep-tracks from Dunsford and Winklesea, and two we spoke to said that it was such a lovely day, they thought they'd get there before the crowd."

"Oh dear!" said Tamzin, absently dusting a bundle of her mother's knitting, which ought not to have been touched. "How terrible! I suppose absolutely everyone has seen about them in the paper, and the place will be stiff with pushing, shouting, staring people. It just doesn't bear thinking of."

Meryon was dusting the mantelpiece, picking up the brass clock and Sussex lustreware as he did so. "Well, we rather thought it was no time for sparing too many of us paper-editing, while the hoopoes were being besieged on that scale, so we agreed that Joseph and Roger should stay there, and I should bike round by Dunsford and send Rissa out there, too, before coming down to help you get the paper drafted out for typing. Then you and I go out with old Mr Decks and the telescope after lunch, relieving either Roger or Rissa to come back and get the stencil cut alone."

"Roger isn't much good at it and Rissa can't type at all," said Tamzin, shaking her duster out of the open window on to a bed of blazing orange snapdragons.

"She said she'd like to have a go, all the same, partly so that she can ride out here on Siani, I think. Roger might be more use at the castle if the crowd gets really awful."

"I suppose she can always use one finger and go slowly," Tamzin said. "Finished your side? Good. We've only got the dining-room to do and then we can go."

All the morning they worked on the paper, carefully writing out the items that had been collected for it and spacing them out so that they would, with any ordinary luck, exactly fit the wax stencil that Rissa or Roger would cut out on the typewriter in the afternoon.

"If there's any space over," said Tamzin, "they can fill it

179

up with stylus drawings. We can leave a note about that." She leaned over the goat-bench to sharpen her pencil with an old razor-blade, tidily catching the shavings on a piece of used sermon paper.

"Perhaps I'd better put the first stencil in the typewriter, before we go," Meryon said, "and if we explain to your mother about how it has to be used sideways, to make two pages to a side, perhaps she would explain to Roger or Rissa. They'll have to use two stencils, of course; one for each side of the paper, to make four pages in all. In fact, we could make eight pages, which would really look much better and not use any more paper, if we divided the stencil into four sections instead of two, and cut the printed pages down the middle lengthwise. I'll do a diagram."

And so the morning was spent, on writing and spacing and correcting and thinking of last-minute oddments to fill up unexpected gaps. There were two more advertisements for Sale, Exchange and Wanted column (above which Tamzin wrote in firmly: "Please note: we accept advertisements *only* at our own discretion"); one from Jim which read: "For Sale, two lobster-pots, or would exchange oil-can (with oil)" and one from Mrs Briggs: "Wanted, kitchen scales, spring type, reasonable." Rissa and Roger had managed to get the cream, butter and eggs advertisement from Harbour Farm, as well as various items of west-side village news, but there were still one or two awkward spaces, and Tamzin was forced to hunt out some more verses from her personal notebook, and Meryon to do a paragraph about the Night Sky in June.

By the time the sound of the luncheon gong rang out across the tennis lawn and stable yard and in at the open loft window, all was in order, and Tamzin and Meryon stretched stiff arms upwards and grinned wearily at each other across the goat bench.

Lunch was another of those glorious vicarage garden meals, at which everyone sprawled or sat according to their personalities and soaked in the wonderful June sunshine which seemed, after the day or two of rain, to have settled again into a perfection of summer splendour. The grass was hot under hands and bare legs, the air smelt of drying lawn-mowings and Mrs Sinkin's pinks, and there was still an occasional cuckoo calling his broken notes from across the river.

"It's heavenly, of course," said Tamzin, her face with eyes shut turned up to the sun as she sat with her hands spread on the grass behind her, "especially after anyone's spent the morning shut up in a dusty hay-loft. But I can't help thinking how much better it would have been for the hoopoes if it had poured all the week through."

She decided not to ride out to the castle this time in case even Cascade's slowest steps should prove too fast for old Mr Decks. She need not have worried. It was rather the other way, because Tamzin was not a fast walker (no one ever knew why, since her legs were long and strong) and, once in his stride, Mr Decks swept along over the green Marsh like a galleon over the sea in a rollicking fair wind. This was no trouble to Meryon, who loved a good swinging pace, but for at least half the distance Tamzin was reduced to a kind of hybrid trotting that made her feel about six years old again and rather foolish. Mr Decks made only one concession to youth, and that was to let Meryon carry the telescope, but Tamzin was convinced that this was only a gesture of propriety, and that older Jim would have walked just as fast with it as without it. Glancing breathlessly up at him from time to time, she had the strange impression that he was a kind of glorious symbol of the Marsh and the river and the sea, as if he were a permanent part of them and she and Meryon only temporary dwellers there.

The great advantage of all this gusty striding was, of course, that so little time was wasted on the journey. In only fifteen minutes or so they were near enough to see the pressing, weaving crowd around the castle, and Tamzin began to be so full of apprehension that if she could have gone any faster she would have done so.

It was about half past two when they came near to the crumbling gateway, threading their way through people who were making the recurrent trip between the outer vantage point near the hoopoes' flight-line and the inner position from where the nest-hole could be seen.

At just this moment Hookey's busload would be leaving Dunsford, Tamzin thought despairingly. Down the sheep-track towards Castle Farm a number of cars and motor-cycles and bicycles were parked, but Tamzin and Meryon scarcely glanced at these. Full of anxiety for the hoopoes they went straight inside the castle, Mr Decks followed closely like Moses approaching the Israelites, and there they found Rissa and Joseph gallantly trying to hold the crowds at bay, but with about as much success as a pair of hinds with a hunt. And over all, incredible though it seemed, a hoopoe came flying, and Tamzin saw that a worm was dangling from its delicate, long bill.

"They're still flying! Oh fantastic – I hardly dared hope they would be," she said to Meryon, weaving her way through the people.

Rissa was looking hot and tired and worried. "Oh, I *am* so pleased to see you!" she exclaimed feelingly. "This is a kind of nightmare – like trying to hold a river back, or something. I suppose it's because we're too young. Rodge is doing what he can outside, but nobody takes much notice."

Mr Decks squared his already very square shoulders and stuck his beard out. "No notice, you say? Ah, we'll see!" His shrewd eyes were following the swooping flight of the hoopoe going out from the nest again, and a strange, reverent look came into his expression. "Beautiful, beautiful! I reckon I lived a dunnamany years to see that, and it were wuth all the waiting." He swung round, glaring suddenly at Joseph and Rissa. "So they wunt let 'em be, hey? Worriting of 'em at the nest and that? We'll see."

Tamzin was never quite sure how it was accomplished, but the bare fact was that, somehow, Mr Decks had that castle cleared and completely empty for the hoopoes in less than fifteen minutes. There was a vague impression in her memory of his patriarchal figure striding calmly round the keep in a manner of supreme authority and confidence, and of people slowly moving out of the gateway in perfect orderliness, without any pushing or resistance.

"We didn't mean to hurt the blessed birds, old cock," a fat youth said plaintively, but he went out just the same, as did the woman with needle-heels whose feet were killing her, and the man in a loud check suit who couldn't see what all the fuss was about, and all the many-coloured, many-sized, many-charactered people that form any British crowd.

Straightening the tilted noticeboard Joseph said blankly, "Eh, gorblimey, didjever see the like? I reckon he got Moses and Abraham 'n'all the perishing prophets proper beat, don't you?"

Now, the only human figure that they could see at all was Mr Decks himself, tall and strong and broad for all his years, standing in the frame of the gateway with the sunshine all around him. Tamzin, Meryon, Rissa and Joseph stared at him with wonder and awe and awaited orders.

"Come you out and keep the gateway," said Mr Decks, as a general calling his officers. "Meryon, lad, git and find a good place fer the telescope and wait there. I be going to see about this lot gawping outsider the walls."

He strode away round the bulging outer bastions, cutting through the astonished people like a battleship through choppy water. What Roger thought when the old sailor arrived to relieve his solitary and losing stand no one knew until after the hour and the moment, but Mr Decks's full, compelling voice came back on the south-west wind, and it seemed that the people were compelled.

Everyone well back from the flight-line, the order was, and no one inside the castle walls. No calling and shouting, no rushing about, and if you can't keep your smallest children from yelling you'd better ruddy well take them home, and that dreckly minute. Such was the general decree, and the commander was not one to be trifled with: he saw that he had complete obedience, though this was not difficult because he was a man gifted with authority.

"An' now," he said, in a voice that was calculated to carry without frightening the hoopoes, because it was low and level, "we have with us here a tidy powerful telescope. You c'n see more through this from a distance nor what you'll ever see natural, closer up. Any man, woman or child as'll give promise to goo home immediate afterwards can have a free look. Line up to the east-ard, if you please, and no pushing."

The crowd, almost to a man, began to line up to the eastward, and without any more pushing than was humanly inevitable. The whole thing was quite beyond understand-

ing, especially to the three who had struggled so ineffec-
tually throughout the whole hot morning to persuade that
very same crowd into merely moderate quietness and
consideration for the fabulous birds.

Showing people, one after another, how to focus on the
flowering may tree, where an anxious hoopoe was calling
its name and agitating its sweeping crest, Meryon reflected
on what a supreme leader Jim's father might have been if
he had not chosen to dedicate his life to ships and the sea.

"Eh, blow me if I can see a blessed thing," said a
delicate small woman in the unexpected voice of a
Yarmouth fish-wife.

"You have to hold it perfectly still, on the fence-post,"
Meryon explained courteously. "Oh – and just move your
hand from the front of the lens!"

"If you look through the wrong end everything seems
ever so small, don't it, Dad?" a knowledgeable small boy
piped up.

Such was the astonishing scene that Hookey Galley and
his First Conducted Outing saw when the blue bus tossed
and dipped and rocked up the track a few minutes later,
with horrified sheep and lambs leaping up and scattering
before it like a white bow-wave before a lurching,
bluff-bowed boat.

Old Mr Decks knew all about Hookey's outing, Tamzin
having breathlessly told him every detail on the headlong
walk across the grazings, and he also knew Hookey as a
man. Accordingly, he left Meryon and Roger in charge of
the telescope, as a skipper might leave his first and second
mates on the bridge in an emergency, and strode to meet
the incoming bus. The only thing to do with men like
Hookey was to get your word in first and firmly. Mr Decks
planted himself in the middle of the sheep-track and waited

for the bus to be forced to stop or run him over. He knew where he wanted it parked, and he had a fair idea where Hookey wanted to park it, but even men like Hookey do not lightly run a person over. Not very much could be heard of their meeting by either the gate-watchers or the telescope-minders, but there was obviously an immediate opening clash about the parking of the bus.

"Hookey wants to bring it closer," said Rissa in the gateway, "to save his customers walking, but Mr Decks won't budge an inch."

"Never mind," said Tamzin, not even looking, "the hoopoes are still flying; isn't it marvellous? It's like a kind of miracle that God has granted us, after the awfulness of our putting them in the paper."

"He's getting the best of the parking battle – look!" said Rissa excitedly. "Hookey's putting it where Mr Decks said. I suppose he didn't want to have a scene in front of his party."

"Now see what happens about the rest of it," said Joseph grimly. "Well, we'll flipping well hold the gate, whatever happens," said Rissa, planting her feet squarely. "If they come in, they come in over our bodies or over the wall."

"You're supposed to be going back and doing the stencil – you or Roger," Tamzin exclaimed, suddenly remembering, but there were only the three of them to guard the gateway, and Hookey and Mr Decks were fiercely arguing down there by the parked bus while the Conducted Outing started drifting, all unconducted, towards the castle. It was no time for thinking about the *Westling News* – no time at all.

Meryon and Roger were busy with the telescope, marshalling the crush of people, focusing the lenses, politely but firmly sending on the ones who had looked for

186

long enough or who were trying to look twice. They hardly had time to take notice of the new diversion, but to the guarders of the gateway it was an anxious interval in which no one could say who would gain the ascendency; Hookey or Mr Decks or even the straggling party itself. There was Mr Decks, ignoring Hookey now and directing the people to move in an orderly manner to the rear of those awaiting their turn with the telescope, while Hookey angrily urged them to take no notice but come with him straight to the nest itself. The party seemed to hesitate, some veering one way and some another; one small child setting up a lonely wail because Father had gone castlewards and Mother had not ("Come back *here*, Bert, and bring our Lucy. Didn't you hear the gentleman say we wasn't allowed at the castle? Though I must say I wouldn't've wasted all that money if I'd known.") and all the time the hoopoes went on flying, anxious and nervous now, as anyone could see by their short, uneasy flights and restless crests, but still flying and still bringing food for their young.

"What shall we do if they rush the gate?" Tamzin asked, watching the divided members of the Outing drifting this way and that, like sheep who have lost a leader.

"Link arms and grab the hinge-bolts and hope for the best," said Rissa valiantly. And for a time it seemed as if that might even yet be necessary, while the two strong wills of Hookey and old Mr Decks strove for the dominance of the party. But after a nasty minute or two Joseph started grinning slowly.

"We wunt need to! The old man he done beaten Hookey down. I reckoned he would!"

"Hey, look!" said Tamzin.

Rissa grinned. "I must say it's worth a week of French verbs to see Hookey's own outing meekly following Mr

Decks while Hookey rants and raves on the outside of the wall, and nobody listening to a word he says!"

"He's the better man is Mr Decks, that's what," said Joseph glowingly. "Cor, blessed if I ever saw the like, and that's a fact, though I been all round the world in my time. Took Hookey's outing right out of his hands, he did. Just look at him now!"

Tamzin sighed a sudden breath of relief and thankfulness and began immediately thinking of their next responsibility. "Really," she said to Rissa, "you could dash off and get started on the stencils, now. I wouldn't have thought it a moment ago, but now I can't see that there'll be anything the rest of us can't manage, so long as the Prophet is here. For goodness' sake be careful with the stencils, they cost money, but Mother'll show you anything you want to know, and Meryon's put the first one in the typewriter for you, and everything's written out all ready."

"Just look at him lining 'em all up!" grinned Joseph, rubbing his hands zestfully.

Rissa divided her attention between Joseph and Tamzin and the glorious victory outside the gates. "They're always writing about supermen, but he's the first I've ever really seen. Yes, I'm going, and I'll be careful and all that" – she was on the point of flight – "I'll go on Siani."

"It'll take you as long to walk to the farm and catch her," said Joseph, "and then to ride back, as what it'd take you to walk all the way to Westling."

"I know," said Rissa. "Haven't you heard about cowboys? They always walk a mile to catch a horse to ride a mile."

"Oh well," said Joseph, "if it takes you like that . . ."

Tamzin watched Rissa swinging away down the sheep-track for a moment, and then she turned to look at the hoopoes again. "I just daren't *think* of what might have happened if we hadn't brought Mr Decks," she said feelingly.

"Ar, that's a very sing'lar man," said Joseph, staring at him with a great respect as he stood towering between the meekly queuing Outing and its own official conductor. "The only thing I been thinking is, what about tomorrow?"

CHAPTER 21

The Latecomer

In church the next morning Tamzin's mind was no more on the service than it had been the week before. There were two of her favourite hymns and Miss Deeprose played "Jesu, Joy of Man's Desiring" as a voluntary, but all was wasted on Tamzin, who was wondering how capable the telephone volunteers were going to be, on their own at the castle, and whether Joseph was managing to get the whole morning there, and whether he had really been successful in persuading his grown-up brother, Mike, to go with him. It all depended on whether a sow had her litter or not, he had told her, and if these things were unpredictable to farmers, how much less could she make a guess, herself? Meryon and Roger would certainly be there, though probably not Rissa, whose parents liked her to go to church with them unless sheer physical disability prevented her. And Rissa had said that they were not particularly impressed by the hoopoes, either, thinking that an escaped parrot that they had found, years ago in Torquay, was far more exciting.

Tamzin herself had asked if church twice on the following Sunday could be considered as sufficient swap for no church today, but though her father made no rule about it, he did point out that she wouldn't much like to ask God's help to protect the hoopoes if she threw over attending His house in order to protect them herself. So that Tamzin felt there were really no two ways about it, and only hoped that God would understand and not hold it against her because her concentration was so lacking that it could hardly be said to exist.

Would the crowd be as big as yesterday's?, she wondered. And, if so, would her friends be able to control them, by themselves, without either the patriarch or his wonderful telescope? She wondered what the Sunday newspapers had printed about the birds, if anything. The vicarage only took one, and that a very respectable one which might be counted on for discretion, but even that never arrived before one o'clock, and often later.

Tamzin was, in fact, so extremely preoccupied that it was astonishing that she noticed at all a very late comer to the service. The big studded oak door stood open to the summer sunshine, so that there was no loud click of the heavy iron latch – only a shadowy movement during the hymn before the sermon, and the soft grating noise of shoes coming quietly over tiles. In the choir stalls, Tamzin lifted her eyes from her hymn book and glanced unmindfully down the aisle as she was singing, but suddenly her eyes shot open very wide and her mouth stayed open, arrested in the middle of a note, because the latecomer was Joseph Merrow.

Now Mrs Merrow fairly often came to church, whenever she could arrange to slip away from the busy farmhouse, which was mostly in the evenings, but Joseph had had a wild and Godless childhood, and no one had yet been able to get him to enter a church. Mrs Merrow serenely said to the vicar, all in good time, and she did not worry herself, but the sight of him now, not only in church but all by himself, and in his working clothes, was one of the most worrying things that had happened to Tamzin ever since her first terrible mistake in spreading the news about the hoopoes.

She scarcely knew how she sat through the sermon. Each minute of its length she became more alarmed, imagining more and more dreadful things that might have happened to the hoopoes and sent Joseph racing over the grazings to enter a church for the first time in his life – because he knew that she would be there, and that it was the quickest way he could speak to her. By the time the service was really over and she had finally reached the open doorway (restraining herself from running down the aisle) and, standing apart from the rest of the congregation, had heard Joseph's message, she was almost relieved, because it was not any worse than it was. But this was only a reaction to her first wild imaginings: in a minute or two, as they walked down the path together, the full awfulness and implications of Joseph's news began to hit her.

"You mean, you think the young have been hurt or stolen, or something, and not just flown? Are you *sure* they haven't flown? If they had, it would be the answer to our whole problem."

Joseph shook his head. "Me and Mike don't think they could possibly've flown, on account of the parent birds keep flying back and forrards, outsider the nest-hole, and crying something pitiful. Mike, he say if young 'uns fly the parents allus knows and goes with 'em."

"Could they have been hurt, or ill, *inside* the nest?" Tamzin asked anxiously, whirring the pages of her prayer book under her thumb because the noise helped her to think.

192

"No. The nest is dead empty. Meryon been and climbed up and put his hand in."

"He did!" There were not many people who would care to make that climb, up the crumbling surface of the keep wall, and even Meryon, who was an excellent climber, had too much sense to attempt it thoughtlessly. "Oh, Joseph, how awful – how absolutely awful! After all our struggles to save them." She had stopped in the path and turned to stare at him bleakly, and Joseph stared back at her with great pity and sadness, bcause he hated anyone to be upset.

"We looked everywhere afore I come here," he said helplessly. "Meryon said he reckoned as you'd want to come right out, drekly church was over, and not wait dinner. He said he got some sandwiches, enough for two."

"Yes, yes, of course," said Tamzin, "but I'll have to change this dress. Look, you walk on while I change, and catch Cascade and I'll catch you up."

"Aye, aye!" said Joseph, making himself grin at her, but Tamzin could not grin back. The young hoopoes had gone; the whole purpose of all their struggle and hope and anxiety. Almost certainly someone had got at them and callously, brutally, done them harm. But who? And what? Were they still alive somewhere, and if so, where? Tamzin ran down the Main Street with her Sunday summer dress floating out behind her, and never even noticed the ferryman chugging cheerfully past her in his wheelchair, so absorbed was she in the urgency of getting to the castle and seeing the disaster for herself.

There seemed no point, anymore, in going to the ferry hut to try to persuade old Mr Decks to come out with his telescope again. Now that the nest had been rifled, all that they had striven to protect was gone. The two parent birds, bereft of their family, would soon leave the place and be no

193

more seen; perhaps no more seen in England at all.

Running into the kitchen where her mother was making gravy, Tamzin came to a sudden breathless stop. "Oh, Mother! please may I go straight to the castle – the young ones have gone! Joseph came to tell me – they haven't just flown, but something terrible's happened – oh, Mother!"

At once the gravy spoon was dropped and her mother's arm was round her shoulders. "Of course you can, pet. Oh, I am so *sorry*! After all you've done. But don't despair; anything might have happened and things are so often not as bad as one expects. Look, while you change I'll knock up a few sandwiches for you, and some fruit."

"Mother, darling!" Tamzin gave her hand a squeeze and dashed away upstairs.

Cascade was not often caught in such flying haste as he was on this Sunday, nor ridden away bareback and without so much as a touch with brush or hoof-pick. But he was a wise pony who took things as he found them, and presently he and Tamzin were drumming fast across the emerald grazings, with the wind in their faces and astonished sheep standing staring at them through cold, amber-ringed eyes.

Long before she reached the castle she saw that people were standing around it again; not as many as on the day before, but this was probably because it was the dinner hour, and the crowds would certainly thicken as the afternoon moved on. But did it matter any more? Did anything matter to the hoopoes, now, except finding their young and seeing that they were unharmed? And though, as any thinking person knew, miracles did happen, it seemed a very small hope that one would happen now to Westling's hoopoes.

Joseph had covered a lot of ground while Tamzin was getting ready to start, and she did not catch him up until they were nearly at the post-and-rail fence, close to the castle, where she threw herself off her pony and tied him up. Cascade blew through his nostrils and shook himself before turning to stare with mild dark eyes and forward flicked ears at Tamzin and Joseph running towards the castle; and then he sighed again and began nosing down at the grass which was always a pleasant change for him from the paddock grazing he knew too well.

There were about ten or a dozen people in and around the castle, mostly picnickers who were already thinking about finding a good place to have their lunch.

"How awfully quiet and sensible they seem, after yesterday's lot," Tamzin said, turning into the gateway. "They must be upset, just the same as we are, by what's happened."

"Time enough, yet," said Joseph, with his worldly-wise outlook. "We'll see what happens about three o'clock time. There's Roger, up on the wall. I reckon Meryon's still looking about the place, somewheres."

Meryon was in the low and crumbling vaults, once used for storing ammunition, and he came out, stooping, when he heard their voices. His hair was covered with cobwebs, so that it looked a kind of iron-grey, and he was about as dirty as Tamzin had ever seen him.

"No luck," he said, brushing his hands together. "It's a bad do; a bad do altogether."

Tamzin looked past him, through the doorway into the keep. "Both birds together," she said. "How awful they must feel!"

Meryon glanced up at them. "Yes, they've been just like that nearly all the time we've been here – just flying backwards and forwards and calling, and never going to hunt for food at all, nor ever going far from the nest. It's been wonderful for the sightseers, of course, seeing both together and for such a long time."

"I suppose you've looked everywhere . . ." Tamzin knew they had, but what else was there to say?

Meryon nodded. "Roger's going round the top of the outer wall, now. But if they were anywhere handy, the parent birds would surely know?"

"I lay someone been at 'em," said Joseph simply. Such a solution fitted in with his own experience of human-kind. "Someone what reckoned there was money to be made outen 'em. Like that Hookey fellow," he suggested. "Seems to me he ent the man to let money pass him by, if he can git his hands on it."

"But if Hookey took the young birds," Meryon said reasonably, "he'd only be dishing his prospects with the outings."

"Well, would he, now?" asked Joseph. "You said yourself as things was better for sightseers, the way they are."

"But Hookey wouldn't know that," said Meryon. "I think every one of us expected the parents would desert if anything happened to the nest or the young. And if they'd done that, what would become of Hookey's outings?"

"It all depends," said Joseph stubbornly, "on what he reckoned he could make outen the young."

"Oh well," said Meryon, brushing his hair with his hands, "at present we don't know anything, except that they've gone. We don't even know how many there were. No one ever saw more than one young bird's head in the nest-hole, did they?" He turned to look at Roger, now completing his wall-top tour and waving to them from the seaward side. "Let's have something to eat. We've got a rucksack over in the shadow, there. And afterwards, until

the crowd starts up again, I thought we might explore the
tide-creeks and ditches."

CHAPTER 22

From Whence Cometh My Help

That Sunday was one of the worst days that Tamzin had ever spent. Looking back on it when she was hastily and hopelessly trying to dash off arrears of homework in her attic, sitting at the table in her pyjamas long after she should have been in bed, she remembered it as a long, burning afternoon in which the crowds gathered thick and unruly, to be crowned by Hookey's second outing which stormed the castle riotously, ungoverned and undisciplined entirely. If she had only stopped to think a minute, she might have gone round to the Point for old Mr Decks and his telescope, after all, and at least the hoopoes would have been spared the extra torment of fear by crowding.

No one took very much notice of the five who struggled to keep peace for them, and the heat grew, and the wind dropped, and people pushed and shouted and dropped cameras and fell over small children: and all the time the hoopoes cried sadly, flying distractedly backwards and forwards by the nest-hole: and it was all a long nightmare that finally crashed in a shattering thunderstorm, the rain bouncing down on the stones and stabbing into thin summer clothes. Except for the clamour of the storm and sudden wind, complete silence fell upon the castle as people ran for shelter to the cars and bus and willow trees: there was little shelter in the castle except in the dingy darkness of the low-ceilinged vaults.

The five who had borne the heat and burden of the day did not mind how wet they got. Except for Tamzin who had run to fetch Cascade in case he was frightened, they stood in a group at the gateway and watched the hurried exodus. Dark patches stood out on the shoulders of their cotton shirts where the rain was soaking, and hair streamed down faces in fringes of running water.

Joseph jerked his head back towards the deserted inner keep. "The only ones who don't seem to care a damn for any of it – people or storm – is the hoopoes."

"They're only thinking about one thing," said Meryon.

"Listen," said Rissa, "you can just hear their voices above the wind and rain. I wish they wouldn't keep crying like that; it makes it seem worse."

Everyone looked at her. For Rissa, the practical, the downright and sensible, to say anything so uncharacteristic was really astonishing. Perhaps she was tired, Meryon thought: even Amazons must get tired sometimes.

Thinking back over it all, Tamzin suddenly realised in an overwhelming sort of way just how tired they had all been. Tired not only with the struggle and the heat but with the gnawing sense of worry and anxiety for the young hoopoes, with pity for the parent birds and remorse for having been the cause of everything.

Staring unseeing at her algebra paper, under the light of her bedside lamp, Tamzin began almost to hate the thought of their *Westling News*. She might have been tempted to drop all connection with it, and at once, if it had not been for their agreement to pay Jim's debt, and for the three and a half dozen people who now counted on their copy every

Tuesday. As it was, she had hardly glanced at Rissa's stencils, waiting up in the office to be collected and taken to Dunsford in the morning.

Tomorrow, Monday . . . there would not . . . be . . . so many . . . people at the . . . castle. . . . Here Tamzin's head fell suddenly on to her algebra book and she was soundly asleep. The lamp beside her was still alight, and her alarm clock ticked complacently as alarm clocks do, and it was not until another hour had passed that she awoke with a start, stiff and weary, and tumbled into her bed.

After she had delivered the stencils on her way to school the next morning, Tamzin stood for some time, deep in thought, beside her propped-up bicycle. None of the hurrying passers-by, going to their own work in the town, could have had any idea that Tamzin's mind was being a battleground between duty and temptation. Not that it was really as simple as that, either, bcause what was duty, to start with? As she saw the situation herself, her duty lay distinctly in two different places – school and the castle – and what she was now trying to decide was which duty was the stronger. All the arguments in favour of going to school were perfectly obvious, of course; honour, trust, obligation, the looming imminence of exams. But what of the hoopoes? Mightn't it be just possible that, if she went out to the castle now, when all was fairly quiet there, she might discover something that no one had noticed before? She had to say "fairly" quiet because, although it was a weekday morning and not the proper holiday season, the morning's papers had not failed to mention this new item about the hoopoes. Tamzin had seen them for herself, in Fred Downing's post office as she came to Dunsford, and there had been headlines such as "Disaster Overtakes Hoopoe Family", and "Westling's Hoopoes Lose Their Young", followed by sufficiently detailed paragraphs for Tamzin to realise that reporters must have been among the weekend's crowds. But now, early in the morning and with the sky still heavily overcast after a night of circling storm . . . surely there wouldn't be many people there? And if she were able to sit in some solitary place, quietly watching, wasn't there at least a good chance that *some*thing might come to her notice? And supposing it did, and it led to the solving of the mystery of the hoopoes, then surely that was a much more important thing than one day at school?

"Excuse *me*!" said a rough voice, and a man pushed past her with two big crates of milk bottles. "Gone to sleep, ancher?"

Tamzin looked at him in surprise, then glanced at her watch and saw that it was already past nine o'clock. All right, then, she said to herself, let that decide it. Swinging her bicycle round she headed back down the road to river bridges and the Marsh.

Not wanting to go past Castle Farm, in case of raising the Merrow's suspicions about her not being at school, she took the track across the levels from the second bridge. It was not a good one for cycling, as few Marsh tracks were, and her old bicycle made enough clatter even on a good modern road. Here, on the stony track, the racket was so appalling that agitated sheep went bounding in front of her before she was anywhere near them. Oh dear, she thought, I do seem fated lately to be horrifying the sheep, but it can't be helped.

About a hundred yards from the castle she dismounted and walked on pushing her machine, which she finally left

201

at the post-and-rail fence. She was taking no chances of frightening the hoopoes; rather she was beginning to feel that if she spent all the rest of her time and thought and energy on them, she would still not have paid the debt she owed them.

As far as she could see there were positively no people at all at the castle. It did seem incredible, but there the old fortress was, standing bluff and strong against the stormy sky, lonely and remote as it had ever been and surrounded only by nibbling sheep and polished buttercups and a clatter of flapping jackdaws.

Subdued with apprehension for the hoopoes, Tamzin walked in through the gateway and came face to face with old Mr Decks. She was much more astonished than he was, though neither could have had the least expectation of meeting the other. Mr Decks looked at her sternly.

"Gal, I reckon you should've been in school."

"Yes, I know. But I wouldn't have been able to listen to anything: and I thought that, coming here, I might be able to think of something to help the hoopoes. I didn't plan it," she added earnestly, "I only thought of it at the last minute, and then I just *had* to come."

"I heard about them young birds," said the patriarch, stroking his beard. "I were allus unaccountable fond of birds, though I lay it seem silly in a seaman." Tamzin had a fleeting idea that he was looking abashed, as if confessing to a secret sin. "So when I hears the young had gorn, see, I ups and doddles over for to see what I could see, though properly speaking I shoulda bin doing the ferry."

"You're rather like me, then!" Tamzin said, grinning faintly at him. "We've both played truant, I mean." She glanced back at the sombre stone keep. "Are they here? Are they still staying by the nest?"

"Well, gal, they *wuz* there, but they bin sitting in them willows, sider the ditch, see, and calling pathetic. Gor, you wouldn't think no one'd do a thing like that, now wouldja, gal, to birds as hem pretty as they? Proper pretty and dentical, they are; real shipshape and Bristol fashion. You compare 'em wid they ole jackdaws; 'tis like comparing a trim liddle sailing clipper wid a dirty ole tramp."

Tamzin turned and began to stare at the invincible thick walls, so hard and stark-looking. Though hung with delicate wallflowers and rock geraniums, they had only the look of a warrior with blossoms in his hair.

"I don't know where else there is to look. I thought, perhaps, when the crowd wasn't here, I might see something. . . . It's funny that there's absolutely no one, isn't it, Mr Decks? After all the dozens yesterday and Saturday."

Mr Decks took out his clay pipe and began filling it. "Tis only the young of the day, gal. But even so, them as has been won't want to come agin, most-in-general, and it is a Monday, too, and a sky as black as the devil's weskit."

Tamzin watched him ramming the shag tobacco down and setting it alight, listening all the time to the sad, strange crying of the hoopoes.

"Come you up the grass slope, young 'un, and sit on the wall-top. Happen we mid think of something, with all the Marsh laid out afore us, same as a blessed great chart."

They turned to walk up the steep grassy slope where earth and fallen stone had built, over the years, a ramp to the top of the seaward wall.

"You'll know what it says in the Psalms – you being a parson's daughter: 'I will lift up mine eyes to the hills, from whence cometh my help,'" said the patriarch. "The grazings is the same to a Marshman, gal, as what the hills is

203

to hillmen. I reckon we better set and look at 'em."

For a long time the old man and the girl sat on the broad wall-top, under the torn, ragged sky, and looked down at the sheep-dotted grazings, studded over with willows and thorn trees. Sometimes the old man looked farther, to the long charcoal line that was the dark sea, still troubled after the storm, but Tamzin just stared at the Marsh and the ditches and the long lines of willows, and at the mourning hoopoes flying sadly to the empty nest-hole. And so watching, they presently noticed a small figure come out of the Castle Farm gateway, a dog at heel and a kind of light-coloured box arrangement dangling from his hand.

"I think it's Joseph," Tamzin said, screwing up her eyes, and it was, and he was coming down the sheep-track to the castle. "I wonder what he's got in his hand; something for the sheep, perhaps, such as foot-rot dressing, but it's a big box for that."

"Tidden a box, young 'un," said Mr Decks presently. "'Tis a cage." And after a minute he added, "And it idden empty, neether."

"Perhaps it's a young jackdaw," Tamzin said, "or a pigeon. . . . Perhaps it's – *oh*!" She turned suddenly and looked at Mr Decks with incredulous widening eyes, a great hope crashing round inside her.

The old man stared back at her. "Perhaps it is!"

Together they scrambled to their feet and went running down the grass slope and through the silent castle and out to the grazings. Perhaps Mr Decks could walk faster than Tamzin, but she could run a great deal faster than he could in his age. She reached Joseph well before he did, but long before that she knew it was a young hoopoe in the cage that Joseph carried.

"Oh Joseph, *Joseph*! You've found it!" She was nearly

crying with the shock of relief and thankfulness.

"Sh! You'll frighten it." He held up the cage as she came panting to a stop. "Not that it's all that timid. Astonishing tame, I'd say, same as the parents. Thass half their trouble, I reckon."

Tamzin stared at it in wonder and awe. "It's beautiful! All fully feathered, too. Where did you find it? Was there only one? Shall we put it back in the nest, d'you think? Oh Joseph, may I carry it?"

"The ole man carn' arf run," said Joseph admiringly, as Mr Decks came trotting up the sheep-track. "Thass a very sing'lar man."

"It *is* a hoopoe!" Tamzin called to him. "Look!" and she held up the cage. "I just can't believe it, after all those hours. Let's go quickly and show it to the parents."

"Where d'yer find it, son?" Mr Decks asked, looking at it reverently as he got his breath, walking back along the way he had come.

"Heel, Jock, good dog! Well, blow me if he wassen in the old pigsty," Joseph said, still astonished by it. "That one we never uses, Tamzin – you know."

"But how on earth did it get there?" Tamzin asked incredulously.

Joseph shook his head. "I dunno; beats me. An' Mike, too. We only found him fer the reason that the old sow she had her litter yest'day, in all that storm, and her roof let the rain in, see. Mike and me we reckoned we got to move her this morning, so we set to cleaning out the empty sty. And there 'e were, a-setten in the corner in there, and lifting his crest and looking at us sideways, like. Well, Mike and me we grabbed him afore he knew we was properly there, an Mike done and fetched Mum's old canary cage and we put him in it. I tried him with a bit of bird seed, what Mum got left over, but he wouldn' ate it."

"It was insects the parents brought – and worms and things," Tamzin said, walking carefully with the cage held out in front of her so that she could keep looking at the wonderful creature.

"We did think of digging some worms up," said Joseph, "but Dad he say much better to get him back quick to the parents, what'll prob'ly start feeding him again on the stuff he's used to. So I come."

"Are you absolutely sure there was only one?" Tamzin asked anxiously, looking out to the willows for the parents.

"Certain sure," said Joseph. "We looked around pretty thorough arter we found him, I can tell you."

"There could've been only one in the brood," said Mr Decks. "I never see more through my telescope. And ent you powerful glad to've found one?"

"Oh, *yes*, of course!"

They walked up to the castle gateway where Joseph made his dog lie down under the leaning thorn tree. "Now what? Shall we putten in the nest? Or let him go? Or what?"

Tamzin looked at the young bird anxiously. "It's so difficult, not knowing how it *got* into the pigsty. Whether someone put it there, or if it somehow flew by itself. Whichever it was, the same thing might happen again if we put it back in the nest – especially if it flew there."

"Well, I'm glad about that," said Joseph honestly, "because I just don't see meself climbing that blessed wall, even without a great cage on me back, to say nothen of hanging on by me brows while I gets him out and pops him back insider the hole."

"I think, really, we ought to leave him in the cage," Tamzin said, "where the parents can see him, and feed him. Then we can let him loose when he's bigger and stronger."

"Do you mean to say," said Mr Decks, "as you reckon folks'd leave it be, if so they could reach a hand and grab it up, cage and all, and make off with it?"

Tamzin looked at him bleakly. "Then what?"

"We gotta hang the cage up sider the hole, see. It takes a good climber to get up there, and I lay there ent a dozen such in these parts, nowadays."

Tamzin and Joseph stared up speculatively at the stark, high wall-face, Joseph certain that he couldn't possibly do it, and Tamzin knowing that she couldn't, and both of them wishing and wishing that Meryon were there. But there was no time to waste. The parent birds came less and less often to the nest-hole, now. By evening they might have flown away altogether, and Meryon was at school away in Hastings.

Old Mr Decks read their thoughts as they stood gazing up at the wall, and he made up his mind.

"I reckon I've climbed that ole wall a dozen times when I were a boy in Westling," he said staunchly. "There isn't many as knows every stone and crack in it as well as what I do. Joseph, lad, cut along back to the farm and fetch a hammer and a big, strong nail; and while you're gone Tamzin and me'll have a hunt fer grubs and insecks."

CHAPTER 23

Uneasy Peace

Late that afternoon Tamzin was cycling home again, via Dunsford because the first duplicated edition of the *Westling News* had to be collected and paid for; and, because she was so happy, she was singing a song to herself as she slumped and rattled down the road.

I don't really know why I'm so happy, she said to herself, when I've got it on my conscience that I've been deceitful all the day, and first I shall have to face the trouble at school. But I *am* happy. She began another verse of her song, grinning to herself because the roughness of the road under her bicycle wheels made her sound like a vibrant soprano.

Well, who could help being happy? With the young hoopoe sitting so complacently in its canary cage, high up on the wall, and the parent birds both joyously feeding it and no more desolate crying on the Marshes. And even though a few people had turned up in the late morning and afternoon, there was no unruly crowd such as had besieged the place over the weekend, and those who came had stood quietly and watched the young bird being fed in its cage, as if they were seeing a kind of miracle, which indeed, thought Tamzin to herself, in a sense they were.

She and old Mr Decks had stayed there all the long, dark day keeping guard over the hoopoes, and Mrs Merrow had sent them a packed lunch by Joseph, with remonstrances to Tamzin about her not being at school, and to Mr Decks about gadding around at his time of life, but the packed lunch had been superb.

There was a cheerful feeling altogether in the air now, as she pedalled down the road into the village. The storminess had finally cleared away from the immeasurable Marsh sky – so vast a sky, with no break to its circular horizon, that every mood within it was reflected at once on the lives of all beneath it. Now it was mild and cheerful and milky-blue again, and the wet earth steamed.

That evening, after Dickon had departed with his potato leaves (now very shabby) for the Point, Tamzin faced the inevitable without any more delay and told her parents about all her day, starting with the long moment of indecision on the pavement of Cinque Ports Street.

"But the really awful thing is," she finished soberly, "that I can't truthfully say I'm sorry, because I know I'd do it again if I felt I had to, the way I felt early this morning."

There was a small silence, as there often was while her parents considered a wrongdoing, and Tamzin gazed at them both, wondering what was coming.

"It was very wrong of you, of course," her father said at last, "but you know that. I think the blame was partly mine, though, because I somehow didn't realise you were as worried as you were, and I was keeping away from the castle because it seemed to your mother and me that the more people who kept away, the better. But if you'd *said* how you thought a visit to the castle on a quiet day would help, I would have gone there for you. In fact, I'll go tomorrow, if you like, as well as on the next day, just to prove it."

Tamzin looked at him with a kind of shamefaced adoration, because he was always so fair and honest, and she had been an idiot, as Rissa would say, not to have confided in him.

"You were a bit of a silly!" her mother said, as if reading her thoughts. "But I'd rather you were silly and honest than clever and untruthful, and I'm glad you told us all about it. You'll have to take the full brunt at school tomorrow, of course, so for my part I think we needn't say more about it – don't you, Richard?"

"Except what about doing your homework now, while you think of it," said the vicar, "and not in the middle of the night, when you're supposed to be in bed."

Tamzin rushed to give them both a great hug, first separately and then together, so that they were like one monumental person, and then she dashed into the dining-room to do her homework, and then suddenly, joyfully, remembered that she couldn't have any because she hadn't been to school. All there was left to do now, then, was to ring up Meryon and Roger and Rissa and tell them all about the astonishing day, and then look through the *Westling News*, Number Three, to make sure that all was done properly before delivering them to Smiling Morn and the post office.

It was as well that she did this – though it would have been much better if she had studied the stencils the day before – because Rissa had somehow mistaken a flippant editorial note of Roger's for printer's copy and had included it in the news, so that one paragraph now read: "The swallows under the Sailors' Institute roof are rearing their second brood this summer [and what a good thing that Hookey G. càn't get at them!] to the delight of Mr and Mrs

Albert Clench, the well-known caretakers."

Appalled, Tamzin rushed for ink and a paint-brush, and spent the next half-hour inking out the offending line in every one of three and half dozen copies. And everyone will only be itching to know what's under the ink, she said to herself, but if they discover how to read it after all, it'll only serve Hookey right.

Apart from this, the duplicated copies seemed to be a great success and the answer to all their printing problems. Every single copy was clear and black and easily readable, and though Rissa's typing had been a bit erratic, as you would expect with anyone's first effort, the drawings were perfect. Tamzin folded all the pages, which they now no longer stitched, and wrote the customers' names on them in the top right hand corner before dashing at last up the village with her bundle.

At school the next day, Tamzin's mind was fairly well at peace. She had got over both the awfulness with her class teacher and the awfulness with the headmistress, to whom she had been sent, and she knew that her father was out at the castle with his lunch and some books in a knapsack. By the time Hookey's next outing came round, on the Wednesday afternoon, someone would have thought of something, and meanwhile she was not going to worry any more. Tomorrow there would be a useful sum to take to Mr Henzie, and at this rate the paper would at least soon have paid Jim's debt, if it was also responsible for nearly breaking up the only hoopoe family in all England.

For two incredibly peaceful days the hoopoe situation remained more or less unchanged. All other younger members of the Hoopoe Committee (as they now thought of themselves) were either at school or, in Joseph's case, at lessons in his home and work on Castle Farm; and of the

211

older members, the vicar and old Mr Decks and four staunch voluntary helpers were taking shifts of keeping guard within the castle and Mrs Grey did what she could to put in a word about the hoopoes' need for peace whenever anyone telephoned for information, as they still quite often did.

Hookey Galley slipped in a couple of evening outings as well as his Wednesday afternoon one, taking advantage of this new and unique development at the hoopoes' nest for a fresh burst of advertising, but he knew better than to antagonise either the vicar or Mr Decks and kept his parties in fair order. Many people had made little effort to hide from him their belief that it was he who had taken and hidden the young hoopoe, and though he violently denied this he knew that he was not popular with the pro-hoopoe half of the village.

There was by now a tremendous interest in the hoopoes throughout the village, which was virtually splitting in two because of fierce disputes as to whether they must at all costs be left in peace to rear their young one, or whether more trade and benefit might not be gained for the village by exploiting them for profit. Already several of the pro-profit section had set up stands selling soft drinks, ices, sweets and chocolates to the sightseers, and there was even a stand of freshly boiled Westling shrimps and another of local-view postcards and ballpoint pens, but Mr Grey had been able to see that none of these was set up within fifty yards of the castle or the flight-line. He had also made a litter-basket with hen-wire which he put up in a suitable place with a notice printed out by Tamzin's mother, and he was not above picking up other people's rubbish and dropping it in.

Mr Decks's telescope continued to be a great help in

keeping people from worrying the birds too closely, but he and the vicar were not entirely happy about all this glaring publicity, however well they managed to control it, and each morning they looked carefully at the young one through the telescope, wondering how long it would be before they felt it was safe to open the cage door.

"There he set, as cool as you like, sir," said Mr Decks admiringly. "Never saw such a cool customer, and that's a fact, a-setting preening of his feathers and enjoying of the view."

"Well, he was born to the limelight, of course," said the vicar, "poor little thing. I dare say he *might* be perfectly all right if we let him go now, but I'd like to see a better-feathered tail on him, first, wouldn't you? Just to make sure."

"Jus' to make sure, Vicar, yes," said Mr Decks, agreeing with him. "And by and large, we ent having all that much trouble now. People seems more reasonable, like, fer all we've got enough trade stands to look like Brighton beach."

They went together to the gateway to look out for the first arrivals of this mild Thursday morning, and Mr Decks, peering through his telescope down the sheep-tracks, talked about the wildness of his son.

"I do believe, Vicar, in a liddle spirit in the young, you unnerstand, and I never did curb him owermuch, 'cept for a tidy beating now and then time I were younger. But he do fare to be ower reckless, and I reckon he overstepped hisself with that back axle. He bin and put a new one in, see, what drive both wheels simultanient – he say so as he can goo round left-hand corners jus' as fast as right 'uns. But I tellim, he gorn and locked the wheels, that away, and wunt be able to turn at all, time he's finished, as well as

213

what it done to his brakes. But you carsn't tellem; they gotta learn by theirselves, till they grow outen it."

Old Jim's father knew his son, and he knew a bit about back axles, because when Tamzin was cycling home on that Thursday evening she very nearly became involved in a second accident with the wheelchair, and this might have been much more serious than the first because she was on a bicycle herself and not walking, as before.

It happened just as she was approaching the vicarage garden, near Smiling Morn's shop. Seeing that the front drive gates stood open for once, she hesitated in her mind for a minute, nearly going through them and the longer way round the house, rather than having to dismount at the little back gate to open it. But noticing the vicarage cats quarrelling in the damson tree by the back door, she decided she had better do something about them. It was at this exact moment that the ferryman came roaring, at full throttle, round the corner in his chair. At least, he meant to go round the corner but he never did. Old Mr Decks's fears about the back axle were well founded: the wheels were now so firmly related that if they could turn a corner at all it could only be a wide one. To her unspeakable horror Tamzin saw the wheelchair skid out sideways, while old Jim leaned desperately out at the other side, like someone sailing a dinghy in the eye of the wind. Then all in less than a moment, he had charged the double gateway and vanished down the vicarage drive out of sight.

Tamzin held her breath and waited for the crash. She had only to wait half a second. And then everyone was running: Mrs Briggs, who had brought the ironing; Mrs Grey, who had been making treacle scones; Dickon, who had been sneaking fresh potato leaves; the vicar, just back from Cloudesley Castle, and Tamzin herself.

At first it seemed almost certain that old Jim must be either dead or seriously injured, for the wheelchair was in ruins against the porch and Jim was sticking out peculiarly from inside it.

"Oh, be careful!" Tamzin's mother warned Mrs Briggs, who was all for hurling herself gallantly on to the wreckage in case it exploded with the ferryman in it. "He might be badly hurt – we must move him carefully."

The vicar sensibly grasped the folding hood, that had folded with Jim underneath it; and as he lifted it there came a loud explosion, not of petrol as Mrs Briggs had feared, but – oh, joyful noise! – of powerful seafaring language such as surely had never been heard before outside the vicarage front door – or indeed inside it, or anywhere near it at all.

Tamzin's anxious face wavered on the edge of a grin as she said, "Are you all right, Jim? Wow, you did give me a fright."

"Am I ruddy well all right, yew ask, gal?" the ferryman roared, purple in his white-fringed face, "'course I ent all right! Stands to reason. Broke every blasted bone as like as not, and bust me tarnation goo-chair so's I gotta be bed-bound."

But somehow, while he was raging, he was standing on his feet, helped and supported by his numerous rescuers while the ruins of the wheelchair sizzled faintly, like some terrible fried hash that had gone wrong and been thrown to the seagulls. And then, somehow, he was standing by himself amid a quickly gathering crowd that was not sated of sights because of a mere pair of nesting hoopoes, and the astonishing thing was that he was simply not hurt at all. There was not even a visible scratch, or a tear of his clothing, and his sailor's cap was still on his head where the roof had jammed it. But the wheelchair was a total loss.

"Scuppered, scuttled and gorn to the bottom!" cried the ferryman sadly, almost weeping over the pathetic pile of wreckage. "First me bike, the ole *Emma* that was, and now me goo-chair!"

"Come inside and have a cup of tea," said Mrs Grey sensibly,taking his arm.

"I'll put the kettle on, Mrs Grey, dearie," said Mrs Briggs, glad to do something.

"You know, Jim, the fact is you can walk perfectly well," said the vicar, "and I think you're an old humbug, myself, and had far better get on with your knitting. I haven't seen you working at it for days, and just look at that old guernsey."

For half a moment the old man attempted to put on his limp, but changed his mind and, looking squarely at the vicar and anyone else who thought him a humbug, he whipped off his sailor's cap and walked powerfully down the vicarage drive, unaided. All right, then, if he couldn't have the wheelchair he wasn't going to be a ruddy invalid, not to please anyone, even if he had just crashed in pieces at the vicar's front door.

"What you could do, Jim," said Tamzin, following him into the kitchen, "is get the old *Emma* brought back. Rissa's father wants to get rid of her, and I expect she's quite as dangerous as the wheelchair."

The old man glared at her suspiciously, to see if she were pulling his leg, but she looked innocent enough.

"Well," said Dickon in the doorway, hiding his newly picked potato leaves behind his back, "I don't call this much of an accident. Not even any blood at all. I may as well go on looking for Jerusalem."

"You little horror," said Tamzin from the dresser where

she was getting cups and saucers, but Dickon had gone.

CHAPTER 24

Into the Eye of the Sun

That Thursday, which had looked like being the third in the days of peace for the hoopoes, in fact was not. The morning and afternoon had been peaceful enough, it was true, and when the vicar had departed at tea-time, leaving old Mr Decks and Joseph in charge for the evening, all had still looked well and in order.

The only contact the vicarage itself had had with the matter was in the arrival of a telegram from a lady in Yorkshire who said that she had successfully reared a young owl and would be glad to rear the hoopoe. But thoughts of mice and rats being offered to that delicate, slender bill were too horrifying to Mrs Grey, who sent back a polite and kindly refusal.

At about five o'clock Tamzin was sent round to the Point to find Dickon and bring him home for his tea. Her father and mother were raking over the shingle of the drive after tidying the wheelchair wreckage.

"Poor Jim!" said Tamzin, pausing before racing off for Dickon, "he did love tearing about in his old goo-chair." Then a sudden dreadful thought struck her. "I say, Dad! Do you know if it was insured?"

"Of course it was," said her father, and then looked up,

twinkling to see the consternation melting off her face. "Ah, I know what was worrying you! Still nearly half the damages to pay off to Mr Henzie, and then Jim smashes up an invalid chair! Bless my soul, you'd need a huge circulation to pay for *that*. However, happily you needn't. But if I were you, my love, and I wanted to adopt someone for protective care, it wouldn't be a wild old river ferryman. Why not try his father? Now that's a sensible man, and very sound on birds, too. He wouldn't let you down."

Tamzin grinned at him affectionately. "Honestly, Dad!"

"Tamzin, darling, dash along for Dicky," said her mother. "It's already past tea-time."

There was no need to go cautiously round Smiling Morn's corner now, and Tamzin never walked if she could run, so that within a minute or so she had found her small brother – not a difficult thing to do while his passion for Jerusalem lasted. He was bending half under an inverted boat, behind the ferry hut, so that it was only his brown corduroy trousers that she saw at first.

"Dicky! It's tea-time and you're to come. Now. It's already past five."

Dickon was scrabbling in the shingle like a terrier after a mole, using one bare hand and a piece of driftwood. At first he only grunted in reply, so that Tamzin began to repeat her message, but suddenly he sat back with a despairing bump and uttered a wail of bitter disappointment.

"I thought I'd really *found* him, and then it wasn't! It looked all so goldy-shiny, too – just the same as if it were Jerusalem, and then it wasn't." Through his tears he stared at his clutched fist that he was opening with anguished sobs to show Tamzin. "That's all it was – and I thought it was

219

Jerusalem, but it wasn't."

In the middle of his hot, sandy palm Tamzin saw a small shining golden ring: not like a finger-ring at all, but delicately twisted, like a fairy person's rope.

"But Dicky! It looks like a proper golden ring!" She picked it up and looked at it closely, turning it about in her fingers. And then she exclaimed in sudden awe, "It *is* gold, Dicky! Look, there's the hallmark; a crown, and 22, and an anchor. I think it's an *ear*-ring. Oh, you lucky boy! Fancy finding a real golden ear-ring!"

"I'd much rather it had been Jerusalem," he sniffed sorrowfully. "But I don't think I shall ever find him, now."

"I just don't understand you!" Tamzin exclaimed, polishing the ring on her jersey sleeve. "Here you've just found a real gold ring, all by yourself – perhaps it's all *for* yourself, if no one's lost it; it may be really old – and you say you'd rather it had been a beetle."

"Not *a* beetle," said Dickon with sad dignity, "but *my* beetle."

Walking home together in the quiet afternoon, they were passing the Harbour Mast when Dickon suddenly dropped his bombshell, that was to focus all the attention of the Hoopoe Committee back on the castle in a single sentence.

"D'you know what," he said confidentially, having thrust this hundredth disappointment about Jersusalem bravely behind him, "when I was under the boat, watching my potato leaves, Hookey Galley and another man came and sat on top of it, and Hookey said, 'It looks like being a good night for the telly, doesn't it, Bert? Six o'clock at the castle, and I've got a big bus load going out to see it.' Then he said something about having a differenter driver because he had to smarten up for the cameras. I thought it was rather funny, Tamzin, a-cause I thought if you'd known I'd have heard you talking about it. So I thought I'd tell you, though a-course I know I shouldn't listen to people when they don't know I'm there, but I couldn't help it, could I, because I didn't know they were coming?"

But Tamzin had long since stopped listening to what Dickon was saying. Her mind was in a similar state of agitation to the kind that happens in a frying-pan of hot oil when someone accidentally drops water into it.

"Six o'clock! That's only an hour – less than a hour! Dicky! Are you absolutely *sure* he said all that?"

"A-course I'm sure. I always am sure." He sounded injured.

"But Dicky, think of it! Lights, and cameras, and cameramen, and technicians or whatever they call them, and a great noisy van, and ladders up to the nest – oh, it's appalling!"

"I expect he's getting a lot of money from the television people," Dickon said, with a wisdom born of knowing Hookey. "I heard him say it was for advertising pills, and it's the advertising ones that do pay, isn't it? Fancy, pills! Our hoopoes!"

"It's absolutely horrific and dreadful to think of," Tamzin said, swinging quickly in at the vicarage gate, "and we've got to stop it. I don't quite know how, but we've got to."

It was quite hopeless anyone expecting Tamzin to sit down properly to tea and, sensibly, no one did.

"We've got to *do* something, Dad, but what?" She stood with her hand still on the doorknob, while her mother stirred the tea in the teapot.

The vicar stared out of the window, his hands folded on the tea-table in front of him. "Well, one thing we certainly can't do, and that's stop the television unit from arriving," he said.

"You could hide behind hedges an' shoot their tyres," suggested Dickon, coming in with washed hands and a washed ring inside them. "Mike and Jim've got guns."

"Oh, Dad – ?" Tamzin looked at him appealingly. Any plan of action was better than none.

"It wouldn't do," said the vicar firmly. "You'd be had up for assault. Besides, they have a perfect right to televise the hoopoes; it isn't breaking any law."

"Then what——?" Tamzin felt as if she were nearly exploding with the pent-up indecision and need for immediate action. She had opened the door now and was edging through it, her eye on the brass clock above the fireplace. "Only three-quarters of an hour, now!"

Her father turned and looked at her. "You could release the young bird."

"So we could! Oh, Dad, what a perfect solution." Tamzin was almost gone, but shot back round the door again. "You're *sure* it's feathered enough to fly – fly strongly, a long way away?"

"I think so. Yes, I think so. It's a good risk to take."

"Tamzin!" her mother called after her, "you absolutely *mustn't* climb that wall, yourself, whatever happens; and if old Mr Decks is still there, he oughtn't to, either. Can you get Meryon?"

"I'm trying to, now," said Tamzin from the telephone in the hall. "And Mother, while I'm catching Cascade could you possibly phone Rissa and Roger?"

"All right, dear, I'll tell them you're going straight out. Look, put these scones in your pocket. You'll be glad for them, later."

For the second time in this week of strange happenings Cascade was caught in flying haste, bridled without

grooming and ridden away fast and recklessly without a
saddle on his back. Once again the shocked sheep bounded
from his drumming hoofs and stared with round yellow
eyes from the tops of shingle banks. Tamzin didn't stop to
open any gates. Cascade could jump very neatly, though
not particularly high, but this time he jumped high enough
for all the gates across the sheep-tracks, and somehow
Tamzin kept her balance, though she had never before
jumped high without a saddle. This time too, she rode right
up to the castle gateway, jumping down and reaching for
the halter-rope that was tied round Cascade's neck before
he had even bounded to a stop. Then she stood and looked
round her, quickly, to size up the situation.

The thing that astonished her most was that, as far as she
could see, there was absolutely nobody about, until it
ocurred to her that people were probably waiting by the
Sea Road gate for the first sight of the television van. The
odd two or three in charge of stalls beyond the vicar's
boundary were too busy preparing for the evening's trade
to take any notice of Tamzin and her pony. She looked at
her watch – there was twenty minutes to go, and no signs of
anything that might be the van. Two bicycles tearing
recklessly past a line of willows would be Meryon and
Roger – oh, thank goodness for that! – and a running boy
coming out from Castle Farm must be Joseph. She couldn't
expect Rissa yet, coming all the way from Dunsford.

In the castle itself a strange peace had descended. But
the hoopoes were still there all right, flying industriously to
feed their big child high up in its airy cage. Oh – and so was
someone else. . . . Making her quick round of investigation
Tamzin found old Mr Decks, the patriarch, sound asleep
on a grass slope with his head on his lunch-bag and his
telescope beside him. It would be a pity for him to miss the

great event, though he did look very weary. Kneeling down, she put a hand on his shoulder, gently shaking him.

"Mr Decks!"

"Eh, whassat, gal?" He was awake at once, like the old deep-sailor that he was.

"We're going to let the young hoopoe go! Hookey's got a television van coming in less than twenty minutes – that's Meryon and Roger coming in at the gate, now."

"We are, are we?" The old man was on his feet at once, his cap on his head and his telescope under his arm."Vicar'n me thought he were gitten well enough feathered. Come on, gal; Sussex'll remember this day."

Running down the slope to the inner keep they converged with Meryon and Roger running in. Under the high inner wall they stopped and stared upwards.

"I reckon you'll be wanting to do the climb, hey, Meryon lad?" said Mr Decks wistfully, as if accepting the greater reliability of youth though longing to have a final go at it himself.

"I'd rather like to – if you're sure you don't mind?" Meryon didn't say that he thought time was too short for taking any risks, but let the old man think he simply wanted to make the climb himself.

"Go on up!" said Mr Decks. "And be careful, ole young 'un. It's a ruddy awful wall."

"I know," said Meryon, "but only in places, and only particularly in one place. Well, here goes!"

Tamzin hated suspense. She couldn't bear to watch Meryon climbing, and she couldn't bear not to. No one spoke to him, because of dangerously distracting him, and no one spoke to anyone else. Once, when a loose foothold broke away and came crashing down at their feet, Tamzin simply couldn't look upwards for a moment, because she knew that he must be hanging almost by his fingerhold alone. It was only at times like this, and with the Deeproses' bull, when he placed himself in deliberate danger, that she realised how unthinkable it would be if one day the danger was too great. And then, by the sudden release of sighs from everyone else, she knew that he was all right again and glanced thankfully upward.

He was only a foot or so from the hanging cage, now, and round his head the parent hoopoes flew, anxiously crying. The young one in its cage leaned down and looked with watchful eyes, now at its parents, swooping distressfully, and now at Meryon, inching himself nearer and nearer. Far, far below were the five white faces, Rissa's now added to the others, all turned upward and watching in silence.

Meryon's right hand tested its hold, and tested it again; and then his left hand reached out to the cage-door. No one moved below, but the hoopoes dashed closer round his head, their wings brushing his hair.

And then the door was open.

Meryon himself never did see the beginning of this historic, ever-to-be-remembered moment. All that he saw was a burst of glorious pink and black-and-white feathers, like a great flower suddenly opening, as the young bird shot out through the open doorway. After that he had to keep his eyes very closely on the wall because going down was worse than coming up. But the watchers below saw the enraptured union of the hoopoe family in the air; swirling up together like a small, private sunset, before they soared over the keep-wall and away towards the willows.

"They've flown! They've flown!" Joseph cried, and everyone turned to race up the grass slope to the outer wall-top and see where they had gone; only Tamzin turned back, halfway, and went down to the hoopoes' wall again,

225

staring up silently at Meryon feeling his way down. But in a few minutes they were up on the wall-top with the others.

"Where are they? Where did they go?"

"In the willows," said Rissa, pointing. "I hope they get a move on before the van comes."

"They be resting, gal," said Mr Decks wisely, "so's the young 'un can feel his wings."

"People are walking down the track," said Roger.

"Ah. There wuz news got round that Hookey got a do on, this evenin', and folks put off coming till then," said Mr Decks.

"Oh, look! Look over there!" cried Tamzin suddenly. "Is that the television? Three enormous great vans, just coming up past Castle Farm!"

"Hell's bells!" said Rissa, "so it is."

"But the hoopoes!" Tamzin wailed, "they're still in the willows."

"Never you mind, gal," said old Mr Decks. "They'll be far outen sight, dreckly minute, you watch granfer." Standing carefully on the wall-top he raised his hands and suddenly, loudly, clapped them. Immediately, there rose from the willows a small cloud of heavenly pink, all barred with clean black-and-white, and away into the western sky, into the eye of the falling sun, went the Westling hoopoes.

It was the kind of moment when no one can ever say anything. It was indeed historic, and it was glorious and precisely timed to the last ten minutes.

Presently, as the big vans lumbered on up the tracks, it was no longer possible to see the small dark specks against the sun-glare, and the rescue party turned to look at each other and at the enemy implacably approaching. Behind the big green vans was the well-known bus, hired so often and so profitably by Hookey Galley, and hurrying up the

226

track were people on foot and people on bicycles, all anxious to see this wonder from London which was, to many of them, much more exciting than a pair of nesting hoopoes.

"But they won't find anything," said Tamzin triumphantly, "not even the cage. Meryon brought it down with him, and you can take it back for Mrs Merrow, Joseph."

Meryon was staring again into the sun, towards Winklesea and the quiet country behind its tree-crowned hill. "They've gone!" he said, "really gone, far, far away. I'm more glad about that than I've been about anything for a very long time."

"I'm glad about a lot of things," said Rissa. "No more danger for the hoopoes, or worry for us about them, and the *Westling News* doing so well that we'll soon be able to pay – pay——" she glanced suddenly at old Jim's father, "just doing so well, I mean; and now to see Hookey done in the eye! It's worth living for, even if nothing else was."

"Perhaps no one will ever really know how the young one got into the sty," said Tamzin, "and probably it doesn't matter now, but everyone will always remember this day as The Day The Hoopoes Flew to Safety."

"And The Day Hookey Was Foiled," said Roger, trying to see whether he was in the bus or one of the television vans. "I expect all his customers'll demand their ticket money back."

"Tis The Day Peace Come to Castle Farm, too," said Joseph. "We ent arf had a rumbustious time there, with all these ruddy sightseers."

"And now it's finished," Rissa said. "It's like, 'When you come to the end of a perfect day'."

"And even for Dickon!" Tamzin said, suddenly grinning. "He found a real golden ear-ring when he was looking for

Jerusalem, and Dad says it's at least three hundred years old."

"I never heard tell of no one losing a ring in my time," said the patriarch. "I lay it musta bin a pirate's ring, or one of them Frenchies'."

"Father found some initials on it that don't fit anyone in the village now, so Dickon's almost certain to get something for it. He cried when he found it, because he thought it was Jerusalem and it wasn't, but now he's really pleased. Dad will have to report it, of course! but Dicky says he's going to buy a vivarium when he gets the money and some moths' and beetles' eggs to hatch in it, and all that. I sort of half-heard when I was telephoning Meryon."

"I tell you what," said Meryon; "a bloke I know in Winklesea's just found a most gi-normous Elephant Hawk Moth chrysalis, that he said I could have. I'll bring it down and see if Dicky fancies it."

Old Mr Decks touched him on the shoulder. "I know you're skipper of this wall-climbing outfit, ole young 'un," he said, "but the enemy is storming the castle gates. How about we nip down this yur outer wall, see, what's a ruddy main road arter the one you just ascended, and doddle orf home peaceful?"

Everyone looked at him.

"I suppose it would be as well," said Roger, "though I'd like to've seen their faces."

"I got me telescope," said the patriarch. And presently, one by one, they landed lightly thudding on the sheep-nibbled grasses, and the only living thing left on the wall-top was a wind-blown wallflower; but in the castle area below a sound of shouting went up, that was carried even across the wind to the peaceful walkers on the Marsh.